PHOENIX

IRON ROGUES MC

FIONA DAVENPORT

PHOENIX

As the treasurer for the Iron Rogues MC, Beck "Phoenix" Evanson was great with money. But he discovered something worth far more in Lindsay Goss. The feisty college student stormed into the clubhouse accusing the club of turning a blind eye—and flipped his world upside down.

Lindsay wasn't scared of the gruff biker with a calculating gaze—especially when the community center she loved was at stake. But when the real threat came after her, Phoenix proved he wasn't just good with numbers. He was ruthless when it came to protecting what was his.

1

LINDSAY

I'd eaten plenty of boxed mac and cheese in my twenty years, but this one didn't even remotely resemble real cheese. Not even the normal fake stuff. Or smell anything like it. But the boxes were basically the only things in Juniper Grove Center's—the local youth community center—pantry that hadn't expired yet. Even if I had to make them without milk and used some of the pasta water instead.

I stirred the contents of the giant metal pot, watching the pale orange powder swirl through the noodles as steam rose into the hot, sticky air. The kitchen fan rattled in the corner, doing little more than pushing hot air in circles. One of the overhead lights had been flickering for days, and I'd already smacked it with a broom handle twice this morning.

"Miss Lindsay, can I stir next?"

I looked down at Devin, one of the fourth graders in the summer camp program.

He had flour on his cheek from the homemade moon sand we'd made earlier and a grin so wide that the knot in my shoulders loosened just a little.

"Only if you promise not to start a food fight again," I teased, handing him the long, beat-up spoon that had probably been here back when I was his age.

"That was an accident!" he insisted, eyes wide with mock innocence.

"Sure it was."

I leaned back against the counter, watching him carefully stir the mac and cheese as though it were the most important job in the world. And honestly, for this place—for these kids—it really was.

I grew up coming here. Back then, it had seemed huge and full of life, with cheerful chaos and crayon-covered posters on every wall. The staff always had something fun planned, the meals were healthy, and the snacks were plentiful. Some Fridays, we even got pizza. Those were the best days.

Now, the kids didn't get to go anywhere fun. Half the hallway lights were out. The vending machine ate quarters without remorse. And each time I'd been tasked with cooking lunch during the three weeks I'd been back for summer break, I'd had to cobble together a meal from whatever supplies hadn't expired in the pantry.

I still loved the community center and didn't think that would ever change. This place had been my home away from home when my mom had to work two full-time jobs just to make ends meet.

The center mattered to me. And so did the kids.

After lunch, we got everyone settled into the main room with a movie. The projector flickered against the peeling paint, casting faded colors onto a wall that probably hadn't seen a fresh coat in a decade. I ducked into the supply closet, hoping we still had enough paper plates and napkins for snack time later.

No such luck. We were down to mismatched paper towel scraps and a half-empty box of peanut butter crackers that looked like they'd been here as long as the paint on the wall.

I sighed and shut the door with my hip, glancing down the hallway where two lights were still out. I'd reported it last week, but the manager had just mumbled something about taking care of it later.

The vending machine at the end of the hall

blinked with a flickering red error light. One of the
teenagers had kicked it in frustration yesterday after
it stole his only dollar. I didn't blame him.

The art supplies were even worse. I'd nearly
cried the day I opened the cabinet and found nothing
but dried-out glue sticks and a pile of broken crayons.
Which was why I'd done some research on cheap
stuff I could do with the kids and came up with the
easy recipe of combining flour and oil to make moon
sand.

And it wasn't just the little stuff that was a
problem around here. The field trip that was
supposed to happen last Friday was canceled at the
last minute due to a supposed transportation issue.
The kids had been so disappointed, but June had
saved the day by grabbing a bunch of beach balls
from her minivan and coming up with a fun game to
play outside. She was the only employee still here
from back when I came as a kid, and she was just as
nice as I remembered.

Something was wrong, and June was the only
person at the community center who I felt comfortable asking about it.

I wiped my hands on a tattered dish towel and
went looking for her.

She was in one of the back rooms, crouched

beside a crate of board games someone had donated, sorting through them with practiced care. A chipped mug that said *Don't Make Me Use My Teacher Voice* sat on the table next to her, and I smiled despite myself. Some things really didn't change.

I leaned against the doorway. "Hey, you got a second?"

"Sure do," she replied without looking up. "Unless you're here to tell me this Monopoly game is missing half of the hotel pieces. In which case, I already know and refuse to be held responsible. I don't know why people think it's a good idea to donate stuff that's useless. It takes three copies of the same game for me to put together a version the kids can actually play."

I huffed a laugh and stepped inside. "Some things never change. I remember you making a game of us sorting the boxes one time when someone dropped off a bunch of them."

She dusted her hands off and straightened, flashing me a smile. "And I seem to recall that you were the best of the bunch when it came to separating the pieces."

"What can I say?" I shrugged and laughed softly. "Counting is fun."

"Says the math major," she teased, wagging her brows. "But not so much for me."

"Speaking of math...I wanted to talk to you about something."

Her eyes widened, and she pointed at her chest. "If you're looking for help with a summer class from me, you're in big trouble."

"Nah." I shook my head as I dropped onto a chair in the corner of the room. "I knocked out all of my required summer credit hours last year. That's why I wasn't here to volunteer."

"Smart girl." She beamed a proud smile at me and asked, "What can I help you with?"

I gestured toward the hallway. "Everything's falling apart, June. The food is beyond awful. We're always short on supplies. The building is a mess. And the kids didn't get their field trip last week."

June shook her head with a sigh. "I know. It's been a rough summer. We got hit hard after the last round of funding cuts."

"Rough doesn't cover how bad it is." I scrunched my nose and tried to remember a link to an article my mom had emailed me from the local paper a few months ago. "But didn't we get that huge donation a while back? From the Iron Rogues MC? I could've sworn it said they gave fifty grand to the community center to support summer programming."

June's expression softened, but she didn't look surprised. "Oh, right. I remember that. Nice photo op, wasn't it? Big guy in a leather vest, shaking hands with Paul, who acted like we just won the lottery."

"So where did the money go?" I asked, my voice sharper than I meant it to be, especially since my questions were probably better suited to the manager. Except Paul didn't strike me as the kind of person who cared as much as June did. "Because it sure doesn't look as though any of that donation was spent on the kids."

"Every dollar gets stretched across ten needs. Insurance, utilities, staff hours, repairs, admin costs. By the time the programs get their piece, there's barely anything left," she explained.

"That's messed up."

"It's exhausting, but at least Paul is the one who has to deal with all of that stuff while I get to focus on the kids we help. He's the one stuck in budget meetings with the board, trying to make every penny count." Her lips curved into a frown. "I just wish I could do more."

I got up and crossed the room to pat her hand. "Give yourself more credit. A big part of how I got a scholarship to college was the good study habits you taught me."

"Thank you, sweetie."

I gave her fingers a squeeze. "I wonder where the money went."

"It's draining to always be putting out fires. But now that you mention it, I can't remember a time in all my years helping out here when it's been quite this bad," she admitted.

Something shady had to be happening around here. I hated to think about anyone stealing from this place that brought such care and happiness to so many kids who couldn't find it elsewhere, but I also couldn't come up with a better explanation.

"I'm going to see if I can figure out what's going on," I said quietly.

She gave me a tired smile. "You've always been a scrappy one."

"Guess I learned from the best."

I quizzed June a little longer, and our conversation only left me even more frustrated.

Since Paul wasn't here, I decided to do a little digging around. What I found only further convinced me that someone wasn't on the up-and-up. I couldn't confront Paul or the board members with nothing but my suspicions and the small bits of evidence I'd gathered. That left me with only one place I could go to for answers—the Iron Rogues. I'd never been to their compound before, but everyone who lived in Old Bridge knew where it was located.

I wasn't sure what kind of operation they were running over at their clubhouse, but if they turned a blind eye to what their money was doing—or wasn't, in this case—they were about to get a wake-up call.

2

PHOENIX

"You realize there's a wedding happening, right?" Maverick asked, after poking his head into my office. He was the vice president of my motorcycle club, the Iron Rogues.

My eyes continued to scan the spreadsheet open on my laptop as I answered, "Yeah. Just wanted to double-check this real quick. The deadline is tomorrow and—"

"The Mendoza contract?" he interrupted.

I nodded and jotted a note to myself on a sticky pad, then stuck it to my computer screen.

Maverick grunted. "Fucking hell. Get your neurotic ass outta this office and ready to party, asshole. You've been over the budget for that project at least twenty times."

"Wait. I need him for just a sec," a female voice cut in.

A murderous scowl enveloped Maverick's face as he turned to look at his old lady, Molly. At least he wasn't directing that glare at me. I liked my head just fine without any bullet holes in it.

"You need who?" he growled.

Molly rolled her eyes and patted his chest over his leather cut. "I didn't mean it like that."

His expression didn't lighten. "Baby, that pretty little ass is gonna be wearing my handprint for days if you don't tell me what I want to hear."

She sighed. "Relax, babe. I only need you, Maverick. And you damn well know it. Now, may I speak to Phoenix for a second without you killing him and carrying me off to your cave?"

He crossed his arms over his chest, glowering at her while he lifted his chin toward me.

"Thanks," she said with an overly sweet smile that had Maverick rolling his eyes this time.

"I know you don't have much time, but someone here needs to speak with you, and it's pretty urgent."

My mouth curved into a frown. I didn't know what could be so important that it couldn't wait until after the wedding.

Molly wouldn't have brought them to me for

something trivial, though, so I gestured for her to continue. She turned to speak to someone out in the hall, not stopping as she walked inside. "Come on in. Don't worry, these guys are all bluster."

I shot an incredulous look at my VP, who just sighed. Usually, Molly wouldn't say shit like that. Having grown up the daughter of an MC president, she knew how important it was for us to maintain a ruthless reputation.

Then I spotted the person who followed her, and my breath froze in my lungs.

She was on the taller side, but still at least six inches shorter than my six-foot-two. Despite her slender frame, she had delicate curves in all the right places. A purple T-shirt clung to her chest, and faded jeans hugged her legs like a second skin. Her tits weren't big, but they were fucking perfect for my hands. And the curve of her hips was just right for holding while I buried myself inside her from behind. Even though I hadn't gotten a glimpse yet, I had no doubt her ass was just as amazing as the rest of her.

Long red hair tumbled down her back, and soft bangs covered her forehead. The color made her pale skin look creamy and emphasized the adorable sprinkle of freckles over her nose and the apples of her cheeks.

Intelligent green eyes—the color of pine trees in the rain—studied me. Her heart-shaped pink lips pursed, and a flush stained her cheeks. I wasn't sure if the blush was from the snap of annoyance in her gaze or the heat she was trying to hide.

My body roared to life, surprising me since I couldn't remember the last time a woman had caught my interest. And I couldn't help feeling a little smug at the obvious signs that she was just as affected by me as I was by her.

"You're Phoenix?" she asked, in a melodic voice that caused warmth to bloom in my chest.

"Beck," I replied gruffly.

If Maverick's and Molly's stunned expressions were anything to go by, they were just as shocked by my response as I was. We didn't invite anyone to use our real names...unless it was women we were related to or intended to claim.

"Pardon?" the woman asked, blinking in confusion. "I'm sorry, Molly called you Phoenix, so I assumed..."

"Phoenix is my road name," I grunted. "You call me Beck."

"Well," Maverick said after clearing his throat. "We'll leave you two to...talk."

He ended his comment with a grin, and I shot him a withering glance before returning my attention to the woman in front of me.

She watched them leave, then turned her inquisitive eyes back to me. "I'm Lindsay. Um, Lindsay Goss. I volunteer at Juniper Grove. I came to talk to you about the center's finances."

I leaned back in my chair, folding my arms, my gaze steady. "Go on."

She shifted on her feet nervously, then seemed to gather her courage and met my stare head-on. I felt ribbons of pride curling around my heart, and my dick twitched because it was sexy as fuck.

"I think someone's stealing from you," she said bluntly. "Sort of. I mean, not you exactly—but from the donations you guys send to the center." Her green eyes snapped with fire. "I can't understand how you've missed it, unless you've suddenly lost all that legendary financial brilliance I've heard about."

My brow lifted, but I didn't bite. Her sass made me want to smile, but I didn't want her to think I wasn't taking her suspicions seriously. "You've seen something?"

She put her hands on her hips, her eyes

narrowed. "I've seen enough. The numbers aren't adding up. Budgets for programs are supposedly approved, but the supply closets are practically empty. Maintenance work orders are submitted, and the expenses logged, but nothing gets fixed. Field trips are mysteriously canceled—breaking promises made to the children. And don't even get me started on the state of the pantry!"

I nodded slowly, already mentally pulling apart the structure we'd set up. Frustration built inside me with every word she spoke. Even though I hadn't been hands-on with the center in years, it was extremely important to me. To the entire club. And if someone was fucking with it, depriving those kids of a safe place and decent meals and snacks, they were gonna pay.

However, I wasn't one to be easily riled, so I remained calm and queried, "You have any documentation?"

Anything she'd found would be useful in speeding up the process.

She crossed her arms, mirroring me. "I have some notes from people I've talked to. And I took some screenshots of anything budgetary I could get eyes on. I'm not a forensic accountant, but I'm also not an idiot. I double-checked everything before I marched into the wedding and nearly ruined your friend's special day."

"Hunter will survive," I murmured, my mind split between the problem at hand and the gorgeous woman I was quickly coming to think of as mine. "He's got his girl. You're worth the interruption."

Surprise flickered in her expression, and pink bloomed on her cheeks, but she kept going. "I tried asking the manager about stuff I noticed that hasn't been done, but he blew me off." She shrugged. "I don't know anyone on the board, and I doubt they would take my calls. Maybe I'm wrong and paranoid—"

"Relax, baby. I believe you," I quickly jumped in to reassure her.

Drumming my fingers on the edge of the desk, I explained, "We've donated to Juniper Grove for years. Quietly, consistently. But I let the board handle allocation. Stayed mostly hands-off because it was so well run in the past. Clearly, that was a mistake."

"Clearly," she echoed with an adorable huff. Her eyes narrowed on me again, her stare probing. "Now you can fix it."

I met her gaze, letting her see I was taking every word seriously. "I will."

Lindsay's arms dropped to her sides, and she exhaled slowly in a small show of relief.

"Need to head out back," I told her, not bothering to hide my reluctance. "Wedding's startin' in a few."

She nodded and turned, but stopped when I ordered, "Don't go back to the center."

Twisting back to face me, she blinked. "Excuse me?"

"You said it yourself, baby...they're dodgin' questions. Don't know how deep this goes. Someone's skimming off the top, and they figure out you've been poking around, they might see you as a threat."

Stubbornness glinted in her pretty eyes, and her mouth parted. I could see she was about to argue, but I didn't let her.

"Not saying this to scare you," I said evenly. "Just makin' sure you understand how serious this is. People do stupid shit when they're cornered. Until I've traced the flow of every dollar and figured out who the fuck is involved, stay away from Juniper Grove. Understood?"

"And if I don't?" she challenged, tilting her head and causing her red tresses to spill over her shoulder.

I didn't outwardly smile. "Then we'll have to

have this conversation again, and I won't be as subtle next time."

Her mouth opened, then shut again, and she nodded.

Good girl.

"I'll contact you as soon as I know more," I said, standing and walking around my desk. My hands balled into fists at my side to avoid touching her. But I lost the fight and trailed a finger across her bottom lip. Her tiny gasp had my dick hardening to stone. "From now on, consider yourself under the protection of the Iron Rogues. Under *my* protection."

She arched her brow. "I didn't realize I needed protecting."

"Neither did any of the other old ladies," I muttered. "But their men knew better."

"I..." She trailed off as her eyes met my heated gaze.

Cupping her shoulders, I turned her around to face the door, then put my hand on the small of her back. I guided her down the hall and through lounge until we reached the front entrance to the clubhouse.

"I'll see you very soon, baby," I told her, my voice low and smooth. My lips pressed tight to hold back my smile when she shivered. Reluctantly, I held the door open for her. She stepped through, then paused and looked up at me.

"Thank you for taking this seriously. The center means a lot to me."

I wanted to unpack that statement, but someone called my name with an impatient tone. Fuck. "Of course," I grunted. "I'll call you soon."

She frowned. "I didn't give you my number."

This time, I let the smile curve my lips.

"Talk soon, baby." Then I nudged her to get going and watched until she was safely in her car.

As I strolled through the clubhouse to the back exit, my mind was filled with thoughts of red curls, pine-green eyes, and a voice that heated my blood.

"Heard some sweet thing got a hold of your balls, Phoenix," Hunter drawled when I walked past him, reminding me of a conversation we'd had recently. I'd given him shit over being pussy-whipped, and he'd warned me that sooner or later, some sweet thing was gonna own my balls—and I'd be beggin' her to squeeze.

I flipped him off, but one corner of my mouth hiked up. Yeah, Lindsay definitely owned me. And it wasn't gonna be long before she knew who she belonged to.

3

LINDSAY

I felt as though I held my breath all the way to my
car. Not because I was afraid, which would've
made sense since I had just stormed into the Iron
Rogues clubhouse and almost interrupted a freaking
wedding. But no, my reaction was entirely due to
Beck.

The club treasurer wasn't at all what I was
expecting. At least when it came to his looks. His
sharp-edged personality seemed like a perfect fit for
the guy who handled the Iron Rogues' money...even
if he did miss that their donation to the center wasn't
being used how it was supposed to.

He hadn't raised his voice. Hadn't gotten defen-
sive. If anything, he'd looked at me as though he was
trying to decide whether I could be trusted. And

when he finally spoke, his voice was deep and smooth. The kind that made you want to listen even if you didn't agree with a word he said.

And then there was the rest of him.

Tall, tan, and broad-shouldered, with dark auburn hair that curled just slightly at the ends. Scruff lined his jaw, and his hazel eyes had an intensity to them that made me feel like I was being studied. And that he saw more than I wanted him to.

The barest hint of black ink peeked out from under the neckline of his shirt. The tattoo on his left arm was more colorful. Deep red roses with green vines wrapped around the petals stopped at his elbow, and I couldn't help but wonder if he had plans for his forearm.

Even though I'd barely been in the clubhouse with him for twenty minutes, I knew one thing with absolute certainty—Beck was dangerous in every sense of the word. Especially to my panties, which were uncomfortably damp after our little chat.

I'd spent too long just trying to keep my head above water to worry about guys. But I'd never met anyone like him. Beck was too much temptation to ignore.

Especially since he hadn't dismissed my concerns. He'd listened and asked questions.

Promised to look into it. And then, with a level of calm confidence that still made my knees feel a little weak, he'd told me to stay away from the center for now.

I hated that I agreed with him. But for some odd reason, I felt safe with him.

THE FOLLOWING MORNING, I was staring at the ceiling fan spinning slowly above me when I heard Mom's footsteps in the hallway.

She tapped once on my open door before stepping inside with a steaming mug of coffee in one hand. Finding me still in bed, she quirked a brow. "Everything okay?"

"Yeah." I sat up, running a hand through my hair. "Why?"

"It's almost eight, and you're still in your pajamas. Shouldn't you be at the center? Or at least getting ready to head over there?"

I shook my head. "I'm not going in today."

She paused just inside the doorway, her expression softening. "You sick?"

"Nope, I just have an unexpected day off and decided to make the most of it by sleeping in."

That wasn't a lie. Just not the whole truth. I wasn't ready to explain that I'd barged into a biker clubhouse and confronted their treasurer about possible embezzlement. That conversation definitely wasn't going to go over well before my mom's first cup of coffee, and she already had enough to worry about.

She handed me the mug. "Sounds like a good plan. You could use the rest. You've been running yourself hard since school let out."

"I'll do my best to get some more sleep," I promised, flashing her a grateful smile as I wrapped my fingers around the warm ceramic.

She pressed a kiss to the top of my head before padding into the hallway.

I sank back against the pillows and let out a long breath I hadn't realized I was holding. It felt strange not to go to the community center. Like skipping a class I knew I couldn't afford to miss. Beck had been serious when he told me to stay away—and something in his eyes said not to take the warning lightly.

Even though every part of me wanted to march back there and demand answers, I was listening. At least for now.

After Mom left for work, and I finished my coffee, guilt started gnawing at me like a splinter I couldn't stop picking at. Not going in today had felt like the right call—and it still did—but that didn't mean I could just not tell anyone.

Setting my empty mug on the bedside table, I grabbed my phone and pulled up June's number, chewing the inside of my cheek while it rang.

She quickly picked up. "Hey, kiddo. Everything okay?"

My voice was soft as I answered, "Yeah, I just wanted to let you know I won't be in today. Something came up."

"I figured as much after everything yesterday, but I appreciate the heads-up."

I sat up straighter. "What do you mean?"

There was a pause, just long enough to make my stomach tighten. "You didn't hear?"

"Hear what?"

"Paul is in the hospital. Someone beat the ever-loving crap out of him last night." June's voice dropped to a near whisper. "They found him in some alley in town. EMTs had to intubate him at the scene. They're saying he's in a coma."

My pulse thudded in my ears. "Are you serious?"

"You know me better than that. I wouldn't joke about something like this."

"Holy crap," I whispered.

"There's even a rumor going around that it was... you know. A message."

For the briefest of moments, I considered the possibility that the Iron Rogues had done this to him. My stomach twisted with guilt as I wondered if I had set this all into motion by going to their clubhouse yesterday.

But I shook the thought away before it could take root. Beck had every opportunity to scare me off yesterday. He could've threatened me, dismissed me, and thrown me out of their compound. Instead, he'd warned me to stay safe. Plus, leaving Paul in an alley to be found by anyone walking by felt reckless, and Beck struck me as someone who was always in control.

"You think the center will close if he doesn't wake up?" I asked, trying to steady my voice.

"I don't know," June said softly. "But I guess we'll find out soon enough."

I ended the call a few minutes later, but I couldn't sit still. I kept thinking about Paul's complete lack of concern whenever I brought up issues at the center. His attitude didn't sit right with me, but he didn't deserve to be lying in some hospital bed because he sucked as a manager. Unless what happened to him wasn't a coincidence, and his disinterest was due to more than just being bad at his job.

By midafternoon, I couldn't take it anymore. I told myself I just wanted to see if the rumors were true. I needed to know if Paul really was in a coma and if things at the center were about to fall apart even more than they already had.

I finally let my curiosity get the better of me and headed to the hospital. My stomach churned as I walked through the front doors and approached the reception desk.

"Hi," I greeted, forcing a polite smile. "I'm here to check on Paul Langford. He was admitted last night."

The nurse behind the counter didn't even blink. "Are you family?"

"No." I shook my head, then explained, "I'm a volunteer at the community center he runs. He's... he's been a mentor to me."

That was a total exaggeration but had just enough truth for it not to sound like I was lying.

She gave me a long look but must have bought my story. "Hang on."

"Sure."

She tapped on her keyboard and glanced at her computer monitor. "He's in the ICU so no visitors are allowed except immediate family. I can't let you up there, but I can let his sister know you stopped by if she leaves before the end of my shift."

Her offer was kind, but I couldn't bluff my way through a conversation with Paul's sister when I hadn't even known he had one. "That's okay. I don't want to bother her at a time like this, with him in a coma."

"Was there anything else I can help you with today?"

"Um...Did they say what happened to him?"

"I can't really give you any medical information due to HIPAA rules." Her gaze darted behind me, then she leaned forward and whispered, "There are two police officers stationed outside his room because it's under investigation."

"Thanks."

I made it halfway to the doors before glancing over my shoulder. I didn't spot anyone looking at me. No alarms were going off. But I couldn't shake the prickling sensation between my shoulder blades that made me think someone was watching me.

4

PHOENIX

I'd spent the morning and early afternoon reviewing the center's financial trail, comparing it with the finances of each board member and the manager. I'd already eliminated the board one by one.

None of them had the balls—or the brains—to pull off a slow-drip embezzlement scheme like the one bleeding Juniper Grove dry. Their finances were mostly clean. Stupid as fuck with their spending, yeah. And I was pretty sure that at least one of them was paying a blackmailer, but I'd address that when this was over.

The payments were easy to spot when you had a head for numbers and money—like I did. Which was how I'd accumulated millions in my bank account.

After graduating from high school at fourteen and college at eighteen, I had put my bachelor's degree in accounting and master's in finance to good use by helping very rich and powerful people with their books. But some of them hadn't been squeaky clean, and I almost ended up under investigation with the FBI. Much to my parents' chagrin since it hadn't exactly made me a good role model for my much younger sister, Melanie.

I was young and needed some direction, so I decided to prospect the Iron Rogues. It had been the best decision I'd ever made. And being a fucking genius when it came to money meant I worked my way up to becoming an officer quickly, being named treasurer around five years ago. Our president was no slouch either, having spent years on Wall Street before coming home and taking his father's place as our leader. Between the two of us, the Iron Rogues never needed to worry about money.

That didn't mean we sat around on our asses. We owned a lot of legitimate businesses and some that were...not so aboveboard. But we kept our activities within the bounds of what was honorable. We lived by our own code, and we were judge and jury when it came to people who fucked with the club.

Which meant that when I figured out who'd

been stealing from Juniper Grove, it wouldn't be the police they'd have to answer to.

Paul had been my first instinct, but I wanted proof to back it up.

By the time I was halfway through cross-referencing the budget line items against the center's actual conditions, I knew it was him. The timing, the sudden uptick in the center's administrative expenses that just so happened to align with funds disappearing from the donation pool.

It was clear that he'd been skimming for at least a year. Maybe longer. The asshole thought he was smart enough to fly under the radar, but he didn't stand a chance now that I was looking into him.

I was poring over the spreadsheets for what seemed like the fifth time, when Deviant barged into my office, scowling like he was about to put a bullet in someone.

"Guy's a fucking ghost," he muttered, flopping onto the chair across from me and tossing a USB drive onto my desk. "Paul Vogel has the digital footprint of a ninety-year-old monk. No socials, no online subscriptions, nothing but his damn work email and the most boring paper trail I've ever seen."

He ran a frustrated hand through his hair before crossing his arms over his chest.

"Yet somehow, he's siphoning money from a youth center," I said flatly, dragging my eyes away from the spreadsheet on my screen to frown at him. "So unless ghosts can make bank deposits, he's hiding something."

Deviant dipped his chin in agreement. "Got one thing, though. He's got an account at another bank. Tried to hide it but was dumb enough to use a fake name variation, and the address linked back to him."

"That explains why every one of the missing dollars I tracked went straight into a personal checking account that didn't appear on any of the center's records," I grunted. "The withdrawals deposited into the unknown checking always happened soon after donation money hit Juniper Grove's accounts. Just enough to keep it from raising red flags so no one would notice."

And I was pissed as fuck at myself for almost letting him get away with this shit.

"Figured you were onto it." Deviant pointed out with a grim nod. "But we still don't know what the hell he's *doing* with the money. The withdrawals are cash. Always from different ATMs. No pattern, no receipts, no digital trail." He ran a frustrated hand through his hair. "Best guess, he's paying someone off or feeding a habit."

I leaned back in my chair, stretching my neck and crossing my arms over my chest. "But there's no sign of any vices showing up in his spending—from either bank account."

Deviant shook his head and rolled his eyes. "You'd think a guy running a scam this long would've at least treated himself to a new car or some better clothes."

He had a point. The greasy little shit still drove a junker, and his wardrobe looked like it came from the dumpster behind a secondhand clothing store. "Maybe he's paying off some dark shit. Debt. Blackmail. Who the fuck knows?"

A crooked smile cut across Deviant's face. "Then again, maybe he's just saving up to buy a personality."

I gave him a dry look that said I thought he was a fucking idiot, then turned my attention back to the computer. Except I didn't really see anything. My mind had wandered to Lindsay again. Like it had constantly since the moment she drove away from the compound.

The way her tits had looked in that snug little tee, gently bouncing as I walked her to the door. Her hips swaying. That pouty mouth that was just beggin' to be kissed. I'd been hard as a rock when she'd challenged me with fire in her green eyes, unconcerned with the fact she was staring down a fully patched member of the Iron Rogues in his own fucking clubhouse. I might have believed her bravado if it hadn't been for the pretty blush that stole across her cheeks. I'd spent way too much time wondering how far that flush would spread down her body when my mouth was on her pussy.

Still, her backbone had impressed me, and her smart mouth was sexy as hell.

I'd ordered her to stay away from the center, but I had a feeling that the girl was too fucking brave for her own good. Too curious and scrappy to leave the situation alone for long. Which meant I needed to check on her sooner rather than later.

"You're not even listening, are you?" Deviant asked dryly.

I tore my attention back to him, not realizing he'd still been talking to me.

He smirked. "Damn, you've got it bad, man."

My expression was deadpan.

Then he grinned. "Heard you told her to call you Beck."

"Assholes who gossip like fucking teenage girls," I muttered.

He tipped his chin toward me. "That's a first-name privilege, and we both know what that means."

"Shut the fuck up," I grunted, my hand tightening into a fist.

Deviant just grinned wider. "Never thought I'd see the day. You lettin' some woman close enough to drop the road name."

"She's not just any woman," I gritted out through clenched teeth.

"No shit. If she was, you'd be sittin' here buried in spreadsheets instead of thinking about red hair and how fast you can get her under you."

I shot him a glare, but it didn't slow him down.

"I get it, man," he said with a shrug. "We all got hit hard when it was the right one. Didn't matter how long it took or how fast it happened. Just meant she was the one who could cut through the noise."

Again, he wasn't wrong. But no way in hell was I gonna admit it out loud.

He leaned back in his chair, lacing his fingers behind his head. "Welcome to the club, brother. Pussy-whipped, obsessed, and one dirty look away from breaking bones for her."

I exhaled through my nose, but the corner of my mouth twitched. "You done?"

"After all the shit you gave me? Not even close. But I'll let it go...for now."

A sharp knock on the door interrupted us, and I looked up to see Fox, our prez, standing in my doorway, his expression tight. "Got something you're gonna want to hear."

My brow drew down, and a fear I'd never experienced before seized my chest.

"Paul's in the ICU," he said without preamble. "Coma. Got the shit beat outta him last night and was left in an alley downtown."

"Fuck," I breathed as relief trickled through my veins at hearing that it wasn't Lindsay who'd been hurt.

However, the fact that Paul had been attacked meant we were dealing with something along the lines of the darker shit we'd speculated about.

"Think it's connected?" Deviant asked, already pulling out his phone.

"Yeah," I muttered. "And we need to know who the hell he pissed off."

Without another word, I jumped to my feet and stalked out of the clubhouse. When I reached my bike, I mounted it and drove out of the compound, headed to the hospital. My fingers itched to call Lindsay—to check if she was safe—but I didn't want her to know about this just yet. I didn't want her to be scared when I wasn't there to remind her that I would keep her safe.

The hospital lot was quiet when I rolled in. I quickly parked, my eyes doing a sweep of my surroundings.

That was when I saw her.

Standing near the entrance, Lindsay had her arms crossed tight against her chest, her gaze darting around nervously.

Damn woman.

I was off my bike and stalking toward her before I even thought twice. She startled when she saw me, but to her credit, she didn't back down. Instead, her chin lifted to a stubborn angle. I refused to think about how cute she was and how her attitude turned me on.

"You got a death wish, baby?" I growled, my hands clenching at my sides. "I fucking *told* you to stay away."

Her spine straightened, and she narrowed her eyes on me. "You told me to stay away from the *center*. You never said anything about the hospital."

I immediately closed the space between us, every muscle in my body coiled tight with frustration and fear-fueled anger.

"You think this is a joke?" I bit out. "Someone beat that bastard into a coma. Don't know who's behind it yet, but I won't let you get caught in the middle of this shit."

"I can take care of myself," she snapped, stepping in closer, like she wasn't the least bit afraid of how pissed I was. I couldn't help the spark of admiration that flickered inside me. "I'm not stupid."

"No, but you're being fucking reckless," I growled, backing her toward the concrete wall of the building. Her pine-green eyes flared as her back hit it, and I caged her in with both arms.

Her scent hit me hard—vanilla and citrus, along with something unique to her—and my semi-hard dick turned to fucking steel.

"Told you, you're under my protection," I murmured, crowding her tighter. "Means you don't go poking around *anywhere* someone might see you as a liability. You let *me* take care of this."

She huffed, but her breath caught. "What are you going to do? Lock me in a tower?"

"Not a bad idea, if that's what it takes to keep you safe." I dipped my head, letting my breath graze her cheek. "And if you don't start behaving, I'll bend you over and spank that pretty ass until it's cherry red. Then you'll *really* learn what protection feels like."

Her pupils flared, her cheeks heated, and her lips parted on a gasp.

"Ummm," she whispered, clearly flustered.

"You get mouthy again," I murmured, lips brushing her ear, "and I'll make damn sure you feel it every time you sit down."

I nearly groaned when her tongue peeked out to wet her lower lip. Then she tilted her head, fire returning to her gaze as she planted her hands on my chest and shoved. When I didn't move so much as a millimeter, she huffed, "You only said not to go near the center."

It was a weak-ass argument, but it drove me fucking crazy when she got sassy.

She could mouth off all she wanted. Every smart-ass word just made her more mine.

I growled, my tone low and full of warning. "Lindsay."

Her lips parted again, but I didn't give her a chance to say another word.

I slammed my mouth onto hers, swallowing her gasp as I kissed her hard, deep, and possessive. Her hands fisted in my shirt, and I pushed her back against the wall so tight there wasn't a breath of space between us.

It wasn't soft or gentle.

It was a claim.

A warning.

A promise.

She was fucking *mine*.

And I would do whatever it took to keep her safe.

5

LINDSAY

One second, Beck glared at me as though I'd said something infuriating. The next, his lips were on mine.

My brain didn't even register the kiss until it was almost already over. Which sucked because I didn't get to give my all to my first real kiss.

I wasn't sure what I'd expected from it, but the way his mouth claimed mine hadn't been sweet. His kiss had been full of a fire that left me breathless when he pulled back, his hazel eyes burning into mine.

My lips tingled, my knees felt shaky, and I couldn't for the life of me remember what I'd said to provoke that reaction. Which was too bad because I already wanted a repeat of that kiss, so I'd love to know which button to push to make it happen again. And again.

"You done arguing now?" he asked, voice low and rough.

My mouth opened, but no words came out.

"That's what I thought." He smirked. "Guess I know how to handle that sassy mouth of yours."

I made a mental note to amp up my cheekiness if getting kissed by Beck was the result. "Maybe it won't work the same next time."

His smile widened as he reached down and laced his fingers through mine. "Let's go. I'm taking you home."

"Wait—"

"It's not up for debate, baby."

I barely had time to think, let alone argue, before he was steering me across the parking lot. My thoughts were a jumbled mess of heat and confusion, but I managed to pull myself together enough that I was about to point out that my car was in the other direction when a van screeched around the corner, tires shrieking against asphalt. Beck stiffened instantly, dropping my hand and stepping in front of me just as the side door flew open and two men in black masks jumped out.

I didn't even have time to scream. The men

moved fast—one lunging toward me while the other circled wide, something long and glinting in his hand. Sunlight flashed off the blade—a knife.

Panic crashed through me like a tidal wave as the closest guy grabbed my arm, yanking me forward so hard that my shoulder jolted. My shoes skidded on the asphalt as I tried to twist away, but he was too strong.

Luckily, Beck didn't have the same problem. His fist slammed against the forearm of the man who grabbed me, hard enough for him to finally release me.

"Get the fuck outta our way," the guy growled.

"Shit, man. Do you see his cut? He's an Iron Rogue. Let's get out of here," his partner yelled, pivoting on his heel to dive back inside the van.

"Fuck," the man who'd grabbed me muttered, his furious gaze darting toward me as he backed away. "Today was your lucky day, bitch. But not next time."

"You won't get another chance at her, mother-fucker." A gun was suddenly in Beck's hand, drawn so fast I didn't see where it even came from.

"Fucking hell," the guy yelled, turning toward the van.

My knees gave out, dropping me butt-first onto

the pavement. Then I was the one screaming when the first shot cracked through the air, the sound deafening and making my ears ring.

Beck didn't hesitate, seemingly unbothered by the noise. Another shot rang out—this time into the front tire of the van, rubber exploding with a sharp pop. The driver floored it anyway, and the vehicle jolted forward, the other three tires squealing as the second man dove for the open side door.

He almost made it inside before Beck fired again, the bullet slamming into the frame of the van just above his head. The guy bumped into the doorframe before falling forward, his partner hauling him inside. The van swerved, metal groaning as it fishtailed and tore out of the parking lot with several more bullet holes in the side, courtesy of Beck's gun.

I was on the ground, breathing hard as I gaped at the disappearing van. My shoulder twinged where the guy had grabbed me, but they were gone, and I was still here.

I was shaken and shivering a little. But at least I hadn't been kidnapped. If Beck hadn't been there to rescue me, I would've been in a heck of a lot of trouble right now.

He was beside me in a blink, holstering the gun like he hadn't just fired a bunch of bullets in a

hospital parking lot. His hands were on me instantly
—skimming over my arms, his expression all dark
fury and hard edges.

"You hurt?"

"I..." My voice cracked. "I don't think so. Just
frazzled."

He let out a low, ragged breath, then reached
down and helped me to my feet. His touch was careful, but his body vibrated with barely restrained
violence. His eyes scanned the street, the rooftops,
and the corners of the lot as though he was expecting
someone else to come for me.

The idea should've been ridiculous, but I hadn't
expected anyone to try to grab me in the first place.

Beck hauled me in close, his arm banding around
my waist as though he didn't trust the ground not to
fall out from under me. His other hand skimmed
down my arm, fingers brushing the spot where the
guy had grabbed me.

"Fuck," he muttered, voice low and tight with
fury. "That bastard put his hands on you."

"I'm fine," I whispered, bracing my palms against
his chest.

His hand snapped up, gripping my jaw just
firmly enough to stop my words cold. His hazel eyes
were molten. Dangerous.

"Don't say that," he ground out. "Don't tell me you're fine after what just happened. You were two seconds away from being thrown into that van."

"But I wasn't," I argued, even as my voice shook.

His touch was protective but commanding. He seemed very close to completely losing control. "If I hadn't been here..."

"You were, though. And you stopped them from taking me." I stroked his broad chest, hoping to defuse the situation. "Although you missed out on your chance to see my ninja moves in action. I was just about to kick some serious butt before you stepped in."

His nostrils flared. "Don't push me, Lindsay."

"What? You don't believe me?" I asked, blinking up at him as innocently as I could.

Beck stepped even deeper into my space, one large hand sliding into my hair and fisting the strands at the base of my neck. His hold wasn't rough, but it was just tight enough that I gasped and went still, my breath catching.

"Now is not the time to give me your sass, baby. Save it for when I have you somewhere safe." His deep voice was gravelly and sent goose bumps up my spine. "If you don't get on the back of my bike in the next ten seconds, your ass'll be red before I let you sit on it."

My jaw dropped. It was the second time he'd threatened to spank me. I should've been furious over him bossing me that way. Insulted. At the very least, offended.

Instead, a rush of heat rolled down my spine, confusing and overwhelming.

I swallowed hard, my knees wobbling in a way that had nothing to do with the adrenaline still in my veins.

"You're being ridiculous," I managed, trying to keep my voice steady. "It's over. They're gone."

"For now." He released my hair but didn't move back, his body still crowding mine. "But I need to get you outta here in case they change their minds and come back."

"We can't just leave." Even if I wanted to, the idea of them returning was now cemented in my brain. "You just fired a bunch of bullets with a ton of people around. The cops must be on their way."

"Your safety comes first," he insisted, nudging me closer toward his motorcycle. "And the Old Bridge PD isn't gonna give me shit for gettin' you behind our gate before calling them. We have too many ties to them for that."

My brows drew together at the mention of the Iron Rogues compound. "You don't have to protect me—"

"Yeah, I do," he cut in, his voice low and final. "We've been over this."

"But...why?"

"Because I take care of what's mine."

I froze.

He'd just called me his.

I opened my mouth, but nothing came out. Beck didn't waste his golden opportunity to get me on his bike. Wrapping his hand around my arm, he led me over to it as though he hadn't just flipped my entire world upside down. Even more than almost getting kidnapped had.

I told myself what he'd said was heat-of-the-moment macho crap. It was just the adrenaline. Too much testosterone.

But my heart was pounding as though it didn't believe me.

6
_____

PHOENIX

We pulled into the compound and around to the back of the clubhouse. I didn't say a word as I helped Lindsay off my bike, then put my arm around her and walked toward the back door. As we passed a couple of brothers and prospects lounging around the firepit and picnic tables, I gave them a terse nod. They were smart enough not to say a damn thing when they saw the storm cloud on my face and Lindsay practically plastered against my side.

I needed to get her alone before I lost my shit.

The moment we stepped inside, I steered her straight to the stairs and up to my room. I lived full-time at the clubhouse. Came with the territory when you were the club treasurer—and a control freak. Unlike the bunk-style rooms most of the guys used for crashes or overnight visits, those who were here full-time had rooms that were closer to a suite. A small sitting area, king bed, desk, and built-in shelves I had loaded with files and books. As an officer, my space also had an attached bathroom. The clubhouse was home, but this was the one place in this building that was only mine. My brothers didn't barge in here like they did with my office.

I shut the door behind us and turned the lock, then watched Lindsay silently as she looked around. Eventually, she faced me with wide, watchful eyes. She was trying to appear calm and collected, but she was practically vibrating with tension.

"Sit," I ordered, voice low, gesturing to the couch. "You need a minute to breathe."

"I'm fine," she argued, her chin tilting in that stubborn way that made my cock twitch.

I narrowed my eyes, making it clear that I didn't believe her. "Humor me."

It wasn't a request, and she knew it. She huffed adorably but padded over to the sofa and sat.

I ran my hands through my hair, then dropped my head back to stare up at the ceiling and sighed. Adrenaline was still pumping through me, and it was making it hard to ignore my desire to expend that energy with Lindsay. In bed. Naked.

When I brought my gaze to her once more, there was a pretty blush on her cheeks, and for a moment, my restraint snapped. I crossed the room in a few steps, bent down, bracing my hands on either side of her head, and kissed her.

It wasn't soft. Or gentle. Or any of the things it probably should have been after what she'd gone through.

It was hard. Consuming. Almost desperate.

I kissed her like I meant it. As though I'd nearly watched her get stolen off the street. Like I needed to taste her just to make sure she was still here. Safe. In my arms.

Her fingers twisted in my shirt, tugging me closer as heat sparked between us. Her breath hitched, her mouth opening under mine, and I inhaled her bewitching scent. I fucking needed her like I needed to breathe.

"Fuck, you taste good."

She was sweet. Addictive. And with a little encouragement, I had no doubt she would be wild.

My hands cupped her face and...

A banging on the door interrupted me.

I growled against her lips, ready to kill the motherfucker on the other side. My forehead dropped to hers as I panted and tried to regain my control.

"Better not be fucking," Maverick shouted from the hallway, his voice too damn amused. "Club business, asshole. Brief the prez before you start breeding her."

"I'm gonna kill him," I muttered.

Lindsay let out a tiny, breathless laugh. "Um... did he say...um. Do you guys always bang on each other's doors like that?"

I scowled at the door as if it would penetrate the hard surface and burn Maverick to fucking ashes. "Only when we know we're interrupting something."

Then my gaze dropped to her stomach for a moment. I decided not to tackle the question she'd been about to ask. Not yet. It would be happening real fucking soon if I had my way, though.

Lindsay giggled again, and I kissed her once more. Fast, rough, and filthy. But over too fast. Just enough to leave her gasping and flushed with intense desire.

"Gotta go talk to Fox." I straightened and walked toward the door but paused to toss one more demand over my shoulder. "Don't wander around without me."

Until she was wearing my property patch, I

didn't want Lindsay running into any of my unattached brothers and giving them the idea that she was available.

When she didn't say anything, I twisted my head and glared at her. She opened her mouth, probably to argue, but I cut her off. "I mean it, baby."

After a second, she gave me a reluctant nod, and I lifted my chin in acknowledgment before forcing myself to turn and unlock the door.

Once I was out in the hall, I leaned against the wall for a second, dragging in a breath as I adjusted myself. My dick was as hard as fucking stone, pressing against my zipper as though it was trying to make a jail break. Last thing I needed was to walk into a strategy meeting looking like I was ready to fuck the wall.

"Relax, asshole. Fucking breathe," I muttered, straightening up and heading for the prez's office.

Fox sat behind his big, modern desk—one you'd expect to see in the executive's office of a financier on Wall Street—with multiple monitors and nothing out of place. He was a neat freak, but only his wife and our VP could get away with giving him shit about it.

Maverick stood on his left, arms crossed, his face impassive.

Whiskey and Deviant were lounging in the small

sitting area on the right side of the office, while Stone sat at the round, wooden conference table on the other side.

"Took you long enough," Stone muttered.

"Was busy," I said flatly, dropping onto an empty chair in front of Fox's desk.

"Yeah, we know," Deviant said with a shit-eating grin. "Mav filled us in."

Whiskey smirked. "Bastard's finally got it bad."

Fox's voice cut through the shit, demanding our attention. "Shut the fuck up. I have a wife and kids waiting, and none of you are pretty enough to keep me here longer than necessary."

The room immediately went quiet.

"Since she's here, and you look like you're gonna flip your shit any minute, gonna assume something happened at the hospital?"

I leaned forward, resting my elbows on my knees. "Someone tried to snatch Lindsay in the parking lot. Van rolled up, masked pricks jumped out. I shot one of the tires and clipped the frame before they peeled off. Had to fire a few rounds. The hospital will have to report it."

Stone didn't even blink, just wrote a note on the legal pad in front of him. "I'll handle the cops."

I nodded my thanks. "Asshole is still in a coma. No help there."

"We should have eyes on him," Whiskey grunted.

Fox nodded and pulled out his phone, making a call. "Send two prospects to the hospital. Then contact the head of the ICU and let him know that they're not to leave Vogel's side until I say otherwise. If the fucker wakes up, I want to know immediately. If anyone tries to get to him, I want them stopped."

He listened for a couple of beats, grunting a response before ending the call. Then he looked back at me. "You sure he's the guy?"

"Positive. Every deposit lines up with donation drops," I confirmed. "And the account he used wasn't tied to Juniper Grove's records. All under the radar."

Deviant nodded. "Pulled his credit report. Paul's drowning. No real assets, no savings, no investments. He's overdrawn most months. The withdrawals are cash, and then he's wiped out."

"Which makes it more likely he owes somebody," Whiskey said, rubbing his jaw. "Or he's paying for something he doesn't want anyone to know about."

"He's still alive, so I think whoever kicked his ass still wants something from him. Putting him in a coma was probably an accident."

"Think he's in with a bookie?" Stone asked.

I shook my head. "Don't think so. The withdrawals are too regular. He'd be scrambling for large payoffs if he was in major debt to a bookie or loan shark."

"Which leaves paying for a vice," Whiskey concluded. "Then why the beating?"

Deviant scratched his chin and rested an ankle on the opposite knee. "Probably pissed someone off, and they were teaching him a lesson."

Fox frowned. "Still doesn't explain why they came for the girl."

I went still, my voice dropping low. "We need to figure that shit out fast. Or I'll put the bastard in the ground. Whatever it takes to keep her safe."

No one argued. It would have made them a bunch of fucking hypocrites since they'd do exactly the same thing for their women.

"She know something?" Stone asked, thoughtfully.

I leaned back and crossed my arms over my chest. "Been poking around. Asking questions. But I didn't think she'd dug deep enough to make waves."

Fox studied me for a second. "We'll figure it out. No one's gonna hurt your girl."

"Damn straight," I growled my hands curling

into fists. Just the thought of anything happening to Lindsay had me feeling homicidal.

"Need to find out where Paul's been going after his withdrawals," Deviant added. "There's no digital trail, so we follow his physical one. ATM cams, traffic cameras, gas stations, whatever. He's cash only, so that's all we've got."

"Start mapping it tonight," Fox said, nodding at Deviant. "Tomorrow, we turn his apartment upside down. He's got physical records, we'll find 'em."

I nodded and stood. "Need to get back to my woman. Make sure she's good."

"Yeah, I bet you do," Whiskey snorted.

"Don't knock it," Stone smirked. "He'll finally be tolerable now that he knows how it feels to be obsessed with his woman."

"Go," Fox said, waving toward the door. "Phoenix, hang back."

The others filed out, leaving the door open behind them. I faced my prez but didn't sit back down.

Fox leaned back in his chair and gave me a look that said he wasn't just my president—he was my friend.

"You want me to send out a vest?" he asked, his lips tipped up at the corners.

A vest. My property patch.

"Yeah," I confirmed without hesitation. "Send it."

I intended to have that patch on her back and my ring on her finger as soon as possible. Then I'd breed her and make damn sure no one ever forgot who Lindsay belonged to.

Fox gave me a small nod. "Figured, but I wanted you to say it out loud. Make sure you were certain."

I didn't reply. I didn't need to. In our world, nothing spoke louder than a property patch.

Maverick lifted his chin toward the door. "Go check on your woman. Deviant'll be digging into shit, and we'll head over to Vogel's place around nine."

"Better find something," I growled. "We don't figure this out soon, gonna burn the motherfucking world down to make sure she's safe."

I stalked out of the office, my blood humming with fury and need.

They'd come after my girl.

And now the whole world was gonna learn what that cost.

7

LINDSAY

I sat on the edge of Beck's bed, staring at the closed door as though it might give me answers. My phone sat in my lap, but I hadn't touched it beyond unlocking the screen and locking it again. Over and over.

There wasn't anyone I could call to talk about this. My mom would freak, my friends from college wouldn't understand, and I hadn't really kept in touch with the kids I hung out with in high school.

Even if I knew who to call, I had no clue what I would say. *Hey, I almost got kidnapped and now I'm hiding out in a biker's bedroom. Also, we kissed, and he called me his.*

Yeah, no. That wasn't a conversation I was

prepared to have. Not with my mom. Not with anyone.

I pulled my knees up and rested my chin on them, hugging them close. My shoulder still ached from where that guy had grabbed me, but I barely noticed because my brain wouldn't shut up. It was spinning wildly.

Who were those guys?

Why did they come after me?

And why had Beck looked like he'd tear the world apart if anyone touched me again?

The questions went round and round inside my head while I curled up on Beck's big bed, his masculine scent surrounding me. I stayed like that until the doorknob finally turned, and I sat up straight as Beck stepped into the room.

There was a tension in his jaw that hadn't been there before. "Everything okay?"

"Could be worse," he muttered, holding his hand out to me. "Save all those questions I see in your pretty eyes for after we eat."

"Eat?" I echoed, my brows drawing together. Food was the last thing on my mind with everything going on, but my stomach betrayed me by choosing now to growl.

Beck's lips curved, and he nodded. "Sounds like it was a good call."

"I could probably eat," I mumbled as he tugged me off the bed and kept hold of my hand as we walked into the hallway.

My gaze darted around the clubhouse as we made our way downstairs and into the lounge. I was surprised by how tidy everything was. With the black leather couches, pool table, big-screen televisions, poker table, and bar, the open space had a masculine vibe, but it was tempered by feminine touches like the red pillows and throw blankets on the couches.

The kitchen was empty when we got there. And huge.

Beck grabbed a container from the fridge, handed me a fork, and pointed at the nearest table.

I sat, and he set the food in front of me. I dug into the Italian pasta salad before I could overthink it. I hadn't realized how hungry I was until the first bite hit my tongue.

My skin tingled and heated, feeling his eyes on me.

"You're watching me eat," I muttered between bites.

He grabbed a couple of Cokes from the fridge,

popping the tab on one before handing it to me. Then he dropped onto the chair to my left and flung his arm over the back of mine. "I like seeing you in my space, enjoying something I gave you."

"Oh." I wasn't sure how to respond to that, so I shifted my focus back to the food.

A thought occurred to me, and I swallowed my bite before asking, "Will you take me back to get my car tomorrow?"

I wasn't excited about being away from Beck, but I didn't want to be clingy. And I couldn't leave my car in the hospital parking lot too long or it would be towed.

"Car's already here, baby."

I swiveled my head around to stare at him in surprise. "How did—"

"Eat, baby," he murmured, pushing the food closer, his expression making it clear that he wasn't open to talking until I'd filled my stomach.

When I was done, Beck took the empty container from me and tossed it in the trash. He didn't ask if I was ready to go back to his room—just tilted his head toward the door.

I followed without a word, too tired to argue and too aware that every step brought me closer to a bed I very much needed.

I lingered in the doorway, unsure what to do now that my stomach wasn't screaming for attention.

"Get some sleep," Beck said, crossing the room to grab a laptop off the desk. "I have work to do."

I probably should've asked if what he had to do was connected to the community center, but now that my belly was full, I was feeling the adrenaline crash. "Okay."

He quirked a brow. "You definitely need some rest if your sass is gone."

I rolled my eyes. "Don't worry, it'll be back."

"Good." He captured my mouth in a deep kiss that left me weak in the knees before stalking over to the closet to grab a big T-shirt that he tossed to me. "You'll be more comfortable in this."

"Thanks."

It was still light outside, but after he left, I used the en suite bathroom to get ready for bed. Then I sent a quick text to my mom.

ME

Hey, I won't be home for a few days. Staying with a friend.

I hoped that would cover me long enough to figure out what was going on. Especially since we hadn't seen much of each other since I'd been home due to both of us being so busy.

Since she always complained about me being too serious, I wasn't surprised by her reply.

MOM

Thanks for letting me know. Have all the fun!

With that done, I walked over to the bed and climbed in, curling on my side with the blanket pulled tight around me. The sheets smelled like Beck —warm and clean, with a hint of something woodsy underneath. It brought more comfort than it probably should when I'd only known Beck for a day.

I thought I'd lie there for a while, eyes wide and thoughts racing. But my body had other ideas. I was asleep before I could second-guess it.

I wasn't sure how much time had passed when I woke up warm. Like really warm. And my whole body shook as if I were on the brink of exploding.

I felt something hot against me and immediately tried to push closer, my hips rotating to hit just the right spot between my legs. Then my eyes fluttered open to meet Beck's hazel ones looking down at me. I blinked hard, trying to pull away, my body heated for a whole different reason now as I tried to hide my face flushed with embarrassment.

"Having a good dream, baby?" He pushed my hair out of my face, even as I tried to bury my head in the blanket.

His fingers slid under my chin, forcing me to meet his heated stare. "You don't need to be shy with me, Lindsay."

I bit my bottom lip, trying to look away, but every time I tried, I found my gaze trailing back to his.

Even with only the moonlight coming in through the blinds, I could make out the outline of his body. The way he fit perfectly against mine under the covers.

"I practically just dry humped you in my sleep," I mumbled.

He twirled a lock of my hair around his finger and smirked. "You could show me your sassy side and ask me for the real thing."

I bit my bottom lip, trying to think of how to explain my predicament. "Um...I've never..."

"Never what, baby?"

Squeezing my eyes shut, I blurted, "I've never slept in the same bed with a guy until tonight, let alone had sex."

"Lindsay, baby. Look at me." His thumb brushed

the apple of my cheek, and I took a deep breath before opening my eyes again. "You mean I'm the first man who's gotten to hold you like this in bed? That if you let me, I'll be the first and only one to ever have you?"

"First and only?" I gulped, looking up at him with wide eyes.

"When I take you, know that you're mine."

He sealed his words with a brush of his lips against mine, lighter than he'd done before. Probably because he didn't want to pressure me into doing anything I wasn't ready for yet. And any other day, I most likely would've backed off. But after what happened in the hospital parking lot, and earlier before he left to meet with his president, I wanted to grab life with both hands. So that was exactly what I did, letting my tongue slide along his as he let out a guttural groan from deep in his throat.

His palms slid down my side, warming me through the thin fabric of the shirt he'd given me to sleep in. Emboldened by his reaction, I slipped my own hands between us and bumped against his dick, which was already hard and stretching the front of his boxer briefs.

I may have been a virgin, but that didn't mean I was completely unaware of what I wanted. But when I ran my fingers down his hard length, Beck didn't react how I expected. He immediately stopped kissing me and grabbed my wrist.

I blinked hard as I tilted my head back to meet his heated stare. "Did I do something wrong?"

He shook his head. "Hell no, baby. Your touch feels too damn good. If you are going to let me fuck you, I need to make sure you're ready for me first. And if you touch me, I'll lose control."

"Oh."

He let go of my hand and unwrapped his body from mine before sliding under the covers.

I couldn't see where he moved, but I felt him as he pressed his hands to my thighs, rolling me onto my back before he tugged my panties down my legs. The fact that I couldn't see what he was doing made his movements even more intoxicating.

There was a whisper of a touch to my thighs. His lips.

Then his finger hooked inside of my already wet entrance.

I gasped, my hips automatically pushing forward as if my body couldn't wait to meet his.

"My good girl was having a very dirty dream." He twisted his wrist with a deep chuckle. "Remind me to have you tell me all about it. Later. After I've made you scream my name at least a few times."

"Uh-huh," I managed to breathe, ready to agree to just about anything with how he was touching me.

"Gonna make you so fucking ready to take my cock," he murmured, breathing on my dripping sex. "I have to taste this pretty pussy."

My legs shook as he dove his head between my legs, with the right amount of pressure in the perfect spots as he devoured me with his lips and tongue.

I gripped hard onto the sheets, my thighs shaking as I felt my whole body light up.

"Beck, yes! Oh yes, I'm going to come," I panted, bucking my hips forward to meet his face.

He didn't stop his movements, only picking up the pace. His fingers and tongue moved in rapid succession as I exploded, feeling my arousal drip down my thighs before he lapped up every last bit of it.

But he didn't stop there. He kept at me, adding his fingers into the mix until I was screaming his name. "Beck! Yes, oh yes!"

I was barely coming down from the high of my orgasms—the first ever given to me by someone else— when he slid upward. He trailed kisses along my stomach, and then my shirt was off, his tongue swirling around each of my pebbled nipples.

His hazel eyes met mine, filled with fierce desire. "Damn, baby. You taste so fucking good. Need to start every day with my mouth on your pussy."

With the pleasure he'd just given me, I wasn't going to argue. "If you keep making me feel like that, I'm on board with that plan."

He chuckled, the stubble of his beard tickling my chest before he lifted his face, kissing me hard. "Ready to take my cock, baby?"

"Yes, please," I panted.

"That's my good girl."

My inner walls clenched at his praise.

He sat up, tossing his boxer briefs to the side. His body looked even better naked than it felt under the covers. I leaned forward, tracing my tongue along the swirling, black lines on his left pec.

"Down, baby," he commanded, nudging me onto my back and sliding just the tip of his dick against my drenched folds.

That was all the warning I got before he started to slide in slowly until he filled me to the hilt. "Fuck, you're so damn tight."

His gaze stayed on mine as he let my body adjust to his fullness.

I spread my legs wider, getting used to his massive size before I gripped his shoulders and moved my hips ever so slowly.

"That's it, baby, take my cock," he encouraged.

I ground against him, any hint of the earlier pain replaced by pleasure. "Feels so good."

"Thank fuck," he groaned, gripping my hips to pull me toward him with each thrust as he picked up the pace.

When my inner walls clamped around his hard length, he growled, "That's it, baby. Give me another one. Come all over my cock."

"Yessss," I hissed.

My whole body hummed as I licked down his pec, retracing the lines of his tattoo. He breathed hard against me, and each time he moved, the glide of his thick dick sent another shock wave straight to my core.

His hand went between us, and I didn't know I could get even more turned on until he rubbed my clit while continuing to pump in and out of me. That was all it took for me to explode, and I cried out his name. "Oh, my... Beck! Yes!"

"Fuck, that's it. Take it all, baby. Milk my cock with that sweet pussy. Yes! Fuck!"

I pumped my hips to meet his, taking in all of him as his orgasm followed mine.

Both our bodies finally stilled, and we stayed connected, our breathing in sync. I never wanted to move from that moment, but Beck eventually detached and got up.

"I'll be right back, baby," he whispered, placing a light kiss on my cheek before he darted to the bathroom.

I heard the spray of the water, then he fumbled back into the dark room, and I felt a warm, wet cloth between my legs. He didn't say anything as he cleaned me up, tossing the towel to the side before he wrapped his arms around me again, my back pressed against his chest.

I was safe and warm, and my eyes drifted closed as if they couldn't stay open anymore.

8
———

PHOENIX

W aking up with Lindsay tucked into my side, soft and warm, was exactly what I didn't know I'd needed. Her bare back was pressed to my chest, her breathing slow and even, her legs tangled with mine. My cock stirred instantly— because how the hell could it not? But I didn't feel an urgency to fuck her.

I felt satisfied.

She was mine now.

I'd marked her.

Claimed her.

And fucked her bare.

The possessive part of me felt smug as hell knowing I was already working on breeding her. If I had my way, she'd be pregnant by the end of the damn week. Maybe sooner. She wasn't going anywhere, not now. Not after the way she'd begged for more, moaned my name, and clung to me as though she never wanted to let go.

Not that there'd ever been a chance in hell I would have let her go before.

I kissed her shoulder, letting my hand trail down her side and curve over her hip.

Her breath hitched slightly, then I heard the smile in her voice when she murmured, "That's a nice way to wake up."

"Mmm," I grunted against her skin. "Better get used to it."

She rolled over to face me, blinking sleepily, and my chest went tight and warm just looking at her. I didn't know how this exquisite creature was mine. Or what I had done to deserve her.

I mentally snorted. Nothing. I would never be good enough for Lindsay. But I wasn't gonna let that stop me from keeping her.

"I have to take care of some club shit," I said with a sigh, brushing a strand of hair from her face. "Probably gone for a few hours."

"Okay," she said softly, but something flickered behind her eyes.

"Lindsay." I cupped her cheek, making sure she

was fully focused on me. "We need to talk about something. I'll never lie to you. But if it's club business, I won't always be able to tell you everything. Some things aren't mine to share."

She nodded without hesitation. "I can handle that. Just don't shut me out, okay?"

My mouth curved as pride lit through me. "Good girl."

Her cheeks flushed like they always did when I called her that, and I kissed her slow and deep. Showing her my gratitude and reminding her who owned her at the same time.

I only meant to make out with her for a few minutes, but the kiss got hotter by the second. When her fingers skimmed down my stomach, I groaned.

"Fuck," I grunted as I pulled back before I forgot what the fuck I was supposed to be doing today.

With an irritated grunt, I forced myself to leave the warm bed and gorgeous, willing woman in it. Then I grabbed a pair of clean boxer briefs from my dresser.

Lindsay's heated gaze dragged down my body, and her brows lifted. "You can't just walk around like that?"

I growled low in my throat and turned toward her. "Keep lookin' at me like that, sass me one more time, and that pretty, sore pussy of yours is gonna get stuffed again until you can't walk tomorrow."

She squeaked, biting her bottom lip as a pink blush stole over her cheeks and spread down under the sheet she was holding up over her tits.

I bent over and took her mouth hard in one last burning press of lips and tongue, then headed into the bathroom for a fast shower.

By the time I got out, she was dozing again, curled up on my side of the bed like she belonged there. Because she did.

A smile curled my lips, and I marveled at the happiness bursting inside me. I'd thought I was happy with my life, but now that I had Lindsay, I realized that I hadn't been living. I'd existed. She brought joy into my life with her musical laughter, sassy mouth, and that hot as fuck body.

I dressed quickly in a black T-shirt, leather pants, my cut, and boots. Then I walked back over to the bed and leaned down to kiss her temple.

"Baby," I murmured softly in her ear. She stirred and blinked at me sleepily, looking tempting as fuck. "I gotta go."

She tried not to pout as she slowly nodded, making me smile. "Fucking adorable, know that?"

Lindsay raised an eyebrow and sniffed. "No

woman wants to be called adorable when they're naked in a man's bed."

A laugh burst from my chest, and I shook my head with a grin. "Relax, baby. You're the sexiest woman I've ever seen. And cute as hell. Somehow, I got lucky enough to have the whole package naked and wrapped up in our bed."

Pink dusted her cheeks again, and she looked pleased with my answer.

I crossed to the closet, grabbed my extra cut, and laid it on the bed beside her.

"If you leave this room, wear this."

She blinked. "Are you giving me a dress code?"

"I'm giving you a fucking warning," I said flatly. "This is nonnegotiable. You wear this cut, and nobody's gonna touch you, look at you, or even breathe wrong in your direction. And if I find out you disobeyed me, we're gonna revisit that spanking."

She smirked, dragging the vest toward her with two fingers. "Yes, sir."

I gave her ass a light smack, a promise and a warning. It wasn't hard, but not soft either. Just enough to make her eyes go wide.

"Don't tease me, baby," I warned, my voice low and rough. "You'll lose."

"I'm not afraid of losing."

I tangled a hand in her hair and held it tight, staring into her eyes with dark intensity. "You should be."

Then I kissed her once more, slow and firm, before smacking her ass one last time and stalking out the door.

Time to get this shit handled and get back to my woman.

Paul's apartment was a shitbox—no surprise there. Three of our enforcers, Racer, Hawk, and Savage, were already inside, tossing the place upside down. Before I joined the search, I scanned the front room, but nothing jumped out at me.

"Found anything?" I asked, stepping around a broken coffee table leg and what looked like week-old takeout. Fucking hell. This guy was a waste of the world's oxygen supply.

"Bunch of junk," Hawk muttered. "Loose receipts, bills, and other random papers, but nothin' helpful. No ledgers. Nothing that gives us a clue to whatever shit he was involved in."

"Wait," Racer called out. He held up a thick spiral notebook. "Found this tucked behind the water heater."

I took it and flipped it open. There were pages full of handwritten numbers, all in columns. No names or addresses. Nothing obvious. Just digits and symbols.

"Could be codes," Savage suggested.

"Could be tracking something." I frowned, scanning the pattern. "Deviant's gonna want a copy."

We took photos of the whole thing and sent them to the tech genius. Then I secured the notebook in my saddlebag before heading out.

By the time I got back to the clubhouse, it was late afternoon. I cut through the side door and followed the sound of soft laughter to the kitchen. I recognized that sweet sound.

There she is.

Lindsay had her hair twisted into a messy bun and was covered in flour as she laughed with Sadie— Hunter's wife and the best damn baker in Tennessee.

Sadie was showing her how to knead dough, her voice warm and patient. Lindsay was smiling like she hadn't been nearly abducted the day before.

That smile settled something deep inside me. I intended to put that happy, satisfied look on her face every day for the rest of our lives.

She spotted me and rushed over, dusting the flour off her hands. "How'd it go?"

"Need a shower after being in that apartment," I

grunted. "But it wasn't a total bust." I raised the note-book and handed it to her. "We found this."

She flipped through it slowly, brow furrowed. "This looks like tracking data."

"Yeah—wait. You recognize it?" It suddenly occurred to me that I hadn't had a chance to really get to know her...other than what her pretty pussy tasted like and how fucking beautiful she was when I was making her come.

"Maybe. Numbers are kind of my thing. I'm getting my degree in statistics."

My brow shot up. "Just when I thought you couldn't be any more perfect."

Lindsay's sweet mouth curved up into a sassy smile. "Perfect? Please. You haven't even seen my spreadsheet skills yet."

I burst into laughter, then smirked as I leaned in, my voice rough against her ear. "If you keep talkin' like that, I'm gonna clear my desk and bend you over it. Club business be damned."

Lindsay's breath caught in her throat, and a shiver shook her body, making me grin even wider. Yeah, that was definitely gonna happen. Soon.

Her eyes dropped back to the notebook, and she cleared her throat. Then her brow furrowed. "Huh."

"See anything that stands out?"

"I'm not sure. Let me try something. Can I see his bank statements?"

"Sure, baby. Let's go to my office." I ignored the bright red that bloomed on her cheeks. If I didn't focus on something else, she was gonna spend the rest of the night being fucked on my desk and every other flat surface I could find.

She called out goodbye to Sadie, who winked and waved. Then I guided her out of the kitchen, through the lounge, and down the hall to my office. She dropped onto the chair at my desk, and I opened my laptop, using my thumb to unlock it before setting it in front of her. Then I pulled up the spreadsheets I'd created with all of Paul's financial transactions.

"Wow. This is even better."

I dropped onto a chair beside her and tossed my arm across the back of hers. Then I trailed my fingertips along her neck as I drawled, "I aim to please."

"Stop that," she whispered, shifting restlessly in her seat, her pretty freckles fading from the flush covering her skin.

I put my lips on her jaw and glided them along the line, then up to her ear. "Is that what you really want?"

She bit her lip and tossed me a disgruntled pout

that was so cute, I couldn't help chuckling. "No," she finally admitted. "Just, um, save it for later."

Chuckling again, I gave her a little space to do her thing. There would be plenty of time for teasing, seducing, and driving her all kinds of wild. We had the rest of our lives as soon as this bullshit was behind us.

She flipped through the pages of the notebook and scrolled through the spreadsheets for a few minutes.

"Yep," she murmured after a while. She pointed at a column of numbers. "Some of these match up to ATM withdrawals."

I arched a brow. "You sure?"

She nodded. "See?"

Pointing at numbers on the screen, then to numbers in the notebook, she showed me how she'd come to the conclusion. I whistled, impressed. "I'll be damned, baby. Nice catch."

Lindsay beamed at me, pointing at another column. "And these look like betting odds. See this column? Looks like wagers and outcomes. Wins, losses."

"That's why he was always broke."

"Yeah," she said slowly, eyes narrowing. "But these two columns still don't make sense."

"Figure it out," I urged her, brushing her hair over her shoulder. "I'm gonna have Deviant send me the information for every betting ring, bookie, and underground game within ten miles of Old Bridge. I'll cross-reference everything, and then we'll widen the net if need be."

She nodded, her whole focus on the numbers, her fingers moving fast over the keys of my computer.

My woman was fucking brilliant.

And gorgeous.

And sexy as hell.

But mostly, she was all fucking mine.

And when we nailed the bastard behind this, I was gonna take her back to my room, strip her bare, and start trying to knock her up all over again.

9

LINDSAY

I'd fallen in love with spreadsheets the first time a teacher showed us how to use them in the computer lab in high school. I knew they could be addictive, but I didn't realize how much fun I could have until I started plugging the numbers from Paul's notebook into one.

At first, it all just looked like a chaotic mess of numbers, scribbles, and shorthand, but the longer I stared at the data and fiddled with the spreadsheet, the more it started to take shape. Some of the numbers matched his bank withdrawals. Some didn't. That part made me second-guess myself each time a theory popped into my head.

Beck was behind his desk, digging into the bookies

and gambling rings the Iron Rogues knew about within a hundred-mile radius of Old Bridge. His presence was steady and grounding, even if I could still feel where he'd been inside me in the middle of the night. It was distracting in the very best way.

"You're humming," he muttered.

"Sorry, I do that sometimes when I'm super focused." I flashed him a quick smile as I tapped my pen against the side of the table where I was working. "You should see me during finals week."

"You always this dangerous with a pen?"

I winked at him and deadpanned, "You should see me with a highlighter."

My quip earned me a low chuckle that made my stomach flutter. Now wasn't the time to straddle his lap and see what kind of reaction I'd get. Or the place since his club brothers had come and gone from the office many times since we'd set up in here. After the way he'd handled me in the middle of the night, I had a pretty good idea of what he'd do, and I didn't want to run the risk of someone walking in on us because there was zero chance I'd notice with how wild he got me.

I forced my attention back to Paul's notebook, frowning as I traced a column of numbers. "There's a second pattern in here. I just haven't figured out what it means yet."

"You will." His voice was steady and certain as though there was no question in his mind that I'd crack Paul's code.

Before I could reply, the door swung open, and Deviant stepped into the office with his laptop tucked under his arm.

"Got somethin'," he announced, not bothering with pleasantries as he stalked over to the table where I sat.

Beck rounded the desk and dropped into the chair beside me, his arm slinging casually around my shoulders.

Deviant flipped the laptop open and turned the screen toward us. "Security footage. We've been watching the banks for camera hits tied to the account withdrawals. Check this out."

Deviant tapped a few keys, and the footage on the screen jumped to life—grainy black-and-white video from an ATM security cam. Paul stepped into the frame, hunched into his windbreaker with the hood pulled low, as though he didn't want to be recognized. He withdrew cash and glanced over his shoulder three times in the span of ten seconds.

"Now watch this," Deviant instructed before

pulling up a video with a different angle from only a few minutes later. "This one's from a nearby gas station."

Paul's car pulled into view, and he got out without pumping gas, parking and walking two buildings over to a run-down mechanic's shop that looked like it hadn't been open in years.

"He didn't go inside," Beck murmured, leaning closer. "Just walked around back."

"Yeah, he pulled this same shit after every withdrawal." Deviant clicked through several more video clips—different days, different banks, always followed by a stop at somewhere odd. A boarded-up bar, an abandoned storefront, a nail salon with blacked-out windows and no signage.

"He's not running errands," I muttered, frowning at the screen.

Beck's arm tightened around me slightly. "Looks like he was being careful. Too aware of his surroundings not to be up to some kinda shit."

"Maybe he was waiting for someone to meet him," I suggested.

Deviant shrugged. "Or was worried about being tailed."

I grabbed my spreadsheet and highlighted two columns of numbers. One of the dates in the first set of numbers matched the videos Deviant showed us. "We already know these are when he's making withdrawals and how much he's taking out."

Beck tapped the screen, right over the column before them. "And you already figured out these are betting odds of some kind."

I clicked on the column to the right of the dates. "But what the hell do these numbers stand for?" Then I moved to the last column. "Or these?"

"Fuck if I know." Deviant shook his head. "The weirdest part is that none of the places repeat. Different spots every time. Only thing they have in common is that all of them are within ten miles of Old Bridge."

As I considered what he pointed out, an idea popped into my head. "What if that's how they're hiding it? They only take cash and move the location around all the time."

Beck nodded. "A moving setup."

"Make sense if they want to stay off our radar," Deviant agreed.

"Different spots, different days, no digital record. Cash withdrawals only. No paper trail, no alerts," Beck listed, rubbing his palm down his stubbly cheek. "It's a solid plan. Nobody would even know they were on Iron Rogues' turf unless you were following a guy like Paul and watching where he went."

"And they were smart enough to keep the locations on the outskirts of town for the closest ones," Deviant pointed out.

Beck let out a low whistle. "Sneaky sons of bitches."

"And organized," I added. "With how much money Paul's burned through, this has to be bigger than some backroom poker game, right?"

Deviant nodded. "Agreed."

"We gotta take them down," Beck muttered, still watching the footage like he wanted to reach through the screen and drag Paul out of it by the throat.

I flipped back through the notebook, fingers brushing over worn paper as an idea niggled in the back of my brain. "We've got odds, dates, dollar amounts. But how does Paul know where to show up? What if the two columns I couldn't figure out are some sort of code for that information?"

Beck quirked a brow. "You think so?"

"Maybe." I flipped through the notebook pages full of dollar signs and numbers until I reached one that had jumped out at me when I was putting them into my spreadsheet. Tapping my finger against the paper, I muttered, "See this? I couldn't figure out what the little dot was doing here when none of the others had one. I thought it was just a mistake. That Paul had dropped his pen or something when he was making this entry,"

Deviant leaned in so he could see too. "And now?"

"What if he skipped the dot on all the rest because it wasn't necessary—he already knew what these numbers meant? But this time, he started to include it because he wasn't paying attention." I grabbed a blank piece of paper and wrote out the odd series of numbers, this time including a round dot and the letter "N" after the first one, adding a minus sign to the start of the second, and then putting another round dot and the letter "W" after it.

Deviant shook his head. "How the fuck didn't I see that?"

"What's the set of numbers for the date on the video we just watched?" Beck punched the digits into the map app on his phone as I rattled them off to him, formatting them like coordinates. After he hit the search button, the address for the gas station popped up on the screen. "You figured it out, baby."

"Which means the column next to the dates are the military times without the colon," Deviant added. "They match up, too."

We checked a few more videos to test our theory, confirming that the times and locations where he went after withdrawing money from the ATM matched up with the numbers listed in his journal when converted to military time and longitude and latitude.

"This is it," I whispered. "The notebook isn't just a record of his bets—it's how they pass along the info to show up at the right place at the right time. Who to talk to. Where to go."

"The bastard is in a coma but left us a damn playbook," Deviant muttered.

"One that screams organized crime," Beck added.

Deviant shut his laptop. "Which means there's someone at the top calling all the shots."

"Exactly," I agreed, adrenaline humming through my veins. "And now we have a way to trace it back to them."

I sat back in the chair, the notebook resting in my lap like it had suddenly doubled in weight. We had locations. Times. A way into something that wasn't supposed to be traceable.

"So now what?" I asked, glancing between Beck and Deviant. "You guys stake out the last entry and hope someone shows since it's dated for tomorrow night?"

Beck flashed me an approving smile. "That's a great idea."

"If we want to know who's running this and find the guys who beat Paul and came after me..." Beck's jaw ticked, but he didn't say anything. "Then someone needs to go inside."

D eviant paced a tight circle in my office, muttering under his breath as he scrolled through whatever was on his tablet. His mind worked fast, and I let him spitball while I stood with my arms crossed, leaning against the edge of my desk, watching Lindsay flip through Paul's notebook again.

"Alright," he muttered, tapping the screen of his tablet. "Next drop is tomorrow night at 2100. Coordinates match a warehouse near the quarry entrance."

"And it's off the main road," I added. "Perfect spot for a backroom game. Quiet. Isolated. No foot traffic."

Deviant nodded. "If someone shows, you going in?"

"Yeah," I confirmed. "If I walk in wearing my cut, they'll assume I've already been invited or told where to go. Not like they're gonna piss off an Iron Rogue until they're sure I'm alone. I'll play dumb and win a few hands."

"Gotta win a lot," he reminded me. "Enough that they think you're a threat to the house take. If they realize you're counting cards, they'll want a talk. That's when we'll get answers."

"I'll play offended and get 'em talking shit."

Deviant gave me a look that was full of warning. "You'll be on your own unless you give the signal. If they get even a whiff that you have backup, they'll clam up and shut the operation down before we learn anything."

I nodded. "I'll push them just enough to piss them off, not enough to get my head blown off."

He barked a short laugh. "They won't take you out right away. They'll try to intimidate you first. Big biker with a sharp eye and a lucky streak? Especially if they think you're alone. They'll want to know how you found out about them."

"Exactly. I want them looking hard," I muttered. "Gives me a reason to push back. Dig deeper."

Lindsay closed the notebook with a snap, her green eyes sparkling. "Or you could bring someone else who can count cards and won't make it obvious. Backup they'd never expect. Like your girlfriend."

I blinked. "No."

She tilted her head and frowned. "No, 'That's too dangerous, baby?' Just a flat-out no?"

I pushed off the desk, my tone hard as steel as I turned to face her. "No as in, not a fucking chance in hell."

Lindsay crossed her arms, the sparkle morphing into a stubborn glint. "You don't even want to hear my plan?"

"I don't give a shit what your plan is," I growled, stepping closer. "You think I'm letting you walk into a goddamn illegal gambling ring—one that nearly got Paul killed and had masked pricks trying to stuff you in a van—just to play wingwoman?"

"I'd be with you—"

"That's not the point," I snapped, cutting her off. "You think I'd let you walk into that den of bastards, dressed up and flashing those pretty green eyes around while you feed me card signals like a fucking movie scene? You really believe I'd be able to focus on a game while every asshole in that room looked at what's mine?"

Deviant stood abruptly. "I'm gonna go, uh... handle setup," he muttered before bolting for the door. Smart bastard.

"You're being an overbearing jackass," she hissed the second we were alone. Her pretty green orbs were burning with angry fire now.

It was nothing compared to the molten rage inside me. "Good. That means I'm doing my job."

"Beck—"

"No." I grabbed her wrist and yanked her forward, crushing our bodies together. "You don't get it. I see red just thinking about you in that place. I have no room left for logic when it comes to you, Lindsay."

Her lips parted, a breathy protest halfway out of her throat, but I didn't let her finish.

I kissed her like it was a punishment and a warning. Like a man who'd burn down the world to protect the woman in his arms.

She gasped, and I grinned against her mouth. "You want to argue, baby? Be my fucking guest. But I'll shut that mouth every time."

"Beck."

Hearing my real name on her lips always sent a surge of pleasure through me, but this time, it flipped a switch in me. It did something dark and primal, making every possessive instinct I had light up at once.

"Bend over the desk," I growled.

Lindsay's breath caught, and her eyes widened. "You're not serious."

I cocked a brow. "Do I look like I'm joking, baby?"

She hesitated for half a second. That was all I gave her.

In one smooth motion, I spun her around and bent her over the desk, her palms catching her weight as I nudged her legs apart with my knee. I yanked down her leggings and panties, baring her to me, and groaned at the sight of her pale, juicy globes.

"You gonna argue with me?" I growled, dragging my hand slowly down the curve of her spine. "Mouth off?"

I punctuated my question with my palm landing on her ass with a sharp smack, the sound echoing through the room. She gasped, hips jerking.

"Then you take your punishment like a good girl."

Another slap, harder this time, right on the sweet spot that had her grinding her thighs together.

"You like this," I muttered darkly. "Getting put

in your place. Bent over my desk with your little ass pink and your pussy soaking wet."

She whimpered but didn't deny it.

I smoothed a hand over her skin before giving her another hard swat, just enough to make her cry out. Then I gripped her hips and slid my fingers between her thighs.

"Still so wet," I murmured. "You gonna behave for me now, baby?"

"I wasn't—"

"Try again," I growled, standing her up and spinning her around to face me.

Her eyes flared, and her voice was breathless. "Beck."

I'd had enough. If I didn't get inside her, I was gonna lose my fucking mind.

"Take off your clothes," I demanded.

When she hesitated, I scowled dark enough to cause wariness to drift into her green orbs. But she was also trembling with desire and softly panting with need.

"Now," I said through gritted teeth. "Or I'll rip them off."

Lindsay stood and peeled her shirt over her head, then kicked her leggings and underwear the rest of the way off.

I yanked her into me for a deep kiss. Sliding my hands low, I gripped her tender ass and lifted her onto my desk in one quick motion. Then I dragged her forward so she was flush against me, the desk biting into her thighs.

"Such a dirty girl," I rasped, palming her soaked pussy. "You like fighting with me? Get you all worked up, baby?"

"You're insane," she breathed, rocking into my hand.

"Maybe. But you're gonna be walking funny either way." I shoved two fingers inside her and groaned at how tight she still was. "This sweet little pussy was made to be bred."

She moaned, her eyes fluttering shut, and I leaned down, biting the side of her throat.

"Gonna fuck you until you forget your own name. The only one I want on your tongue is mine."

I didn't wait.

I shoved my jeans down just enough to free my cock and lined up at her entrance, still holding her on the desk with one arm while I pushed inside with a deep, brutal thrust. A groan tore from my throat at how tight and perfect she felt.

Her walls clamped around me, and she moaned,

her fingers gripping the desk edge as though her life depended on it.

"This is mine," I growled. "No one else gets to touch you. No one else ever will."

She cried out, and I swallowed the sound with a kiss as I pushed her down until she was lying on her back.

I set a hard, punishing rhythm, every slap of skin against skin echoing in the room. Her whimpers turned to cries as I drove into her. Every stroke was rough. Possessive. I grabbed her wrists and pinned them above her head, my hips pounding into hers as the desk creaked beneath us.

"You like this?" I ground out. "My claimin' you like this while you're still arguing with me?"

She nodded, and her lips parted, but she was too breathless to speak.

"That's right. I own this pussy," I rasped, voice ragged. "And you're gonna take every inch. I'm gonna stuff you full of my come until you're bred. You were fucking made to carry my babies."

I reached between us and rubbed her clit, hard and fast. She came with a broken cry, her body clenching around me, and I rammed into her twice more before I buried myself so deep the tip of my cock was touching her cervix. Then I followed her over the edge with a guttural growl, emptying inside her in thick, pulsing bursts while holding her tight.

We were both shaking when I finally pulled back. Her skin glowed, her cheeks flushed, and her breaths came in fast, shallow gasps as I slowly eased out then pulled her against my chest.

"Still want to come with me tomorrow?" I murmured, brushing a kiss to her temple.

She huffed out a weak laugh. "Maybe after I can walk again."

I grinned and kissed her softly. "That's my girl."

Her legs wobbled as I helped her off the desk, then she blinked up at me, her eyes still glazed and her skin flushed pink.

"So, you're not still mad at me?" she asked in a hoarse voice.

I smirked as I pulled off my shirt and slid it over her head before scooping her into my arms. "Nah. I like your sass."

Quickly, I carried her upstairs to our room.

I didn't even make it to the bed before I was on her again.

The oversized T-shirt I'd dressed her in was yanked over her head and tossed aside in a flash, baring her flushed skin and those gorgeous curves that I would never get enough of. I dipped my head to her chest, and her nipples peaked the second my breath hit them. My cock throbbed at the sound of her little gasp when I bent down to suck one into my mouth.

I put my hand on her belly and pushed her until she fell down onto the edge of the bed, lying on her back. Then I dropped to my knees right there on the damn floor. Her thighs parted for me, her soaked little pussy practically begging for my mouth.

"Mine," I growled, locking eyes with her as I pushed her knees as wide as they would go. "You understand me, baby?"

She nodded, her breaths coming in short, needy pants.

"Say it," I demanded.

"Yours," she whimpered.

"Damn straight," I growled before burying my face between her legs like a man possessed. Licking, and sucking, and biting. I fucked her with my tongue until she was writhing and sobbing my name. I was relentless, driving her wild without pushing her over the edge. When she bucked and wiggled, trying to escape the overwhelming pleasure, I held her hips down. Eventually, her legs started to shake, and I growled against her clit. Then I sucked it. Hard.

The way she screamed for me, begged me not to

stop, made my blood run hot, and I nearly came right then. The sounds of her pleasure would play on repeat in my head until the day I died.

Finally, her shudders subsided, and I lifted off her. She was trembling, her body flushed and exhausted—but she still looked at me with need.

I knew exactly what she *needed*.

I crawled over her, dragging my hard length along the seam of her soaked folds, releasing a small burst of come when she gasped and her nipples tightened to diamond-hard peaks.

"Never gonna get enough of you, baby," I murmured, letting her see the deep emotions I felt for her in my eyes.

She blinked up at me with beautiful, trusting eyes and whispered, "Yours."

Fucking right she was.

"You're mine," I said roughly, sliding deep inside her in one smooth thrust. "My girl. My woman. My everything."

She gasped, her arms wrapping tight around my neck as I buried myself in her again and again.

"So fucking tight," I groaned. "Love the way your pussy squeezes me, baby."

I slowed my pace, but kept my thrusts deep as I

kissed her with a reverence I didn't know I had in me.

"That's it, baby," I murmured in her ear. "Take all of me. Let me make you mine in every way. Want to make sure I leave a part of me inside you. Gonna keep you bare in this bed, takin' every inch of me until it happens, 'cause you were made for it. Made for me."

I rocked into her over and over, and her legs locked around my waist, her body tightening with every stroke, growing closer to an explosion.

"You feel that?" I whispered, my mouth hot against her jaw as I trailed kisses over her silky skin. "How full you are?"

She nodded, and her pussy rippled around my cock.

"Gonna breed you, baby," I murmured, my voice wrecked with need. "Over and over until you can't walk. Until you're dripping with me and carrying my kid."

Her nails raked down my back, her breath catching as another orgasm slammed into her. I groaned and dropped my head to her neck, fucking her through it, not stopping until she went boneless beneath me.

Still, I didn't stop. Couldn't. Not until she came

again with a strangled cry, her fingers fisting the sheets.

Finally, I followed, pumping into her with a broken growl, hips jerking as I emptied every drop inside her.

She clung to me, panting and completely wrecked from pleasure.

I kissed her temple, her cheek, her lips. Whispered sweet soft things, with a few filthy ones thrown in because...well, I was still a fucking badass biker.

Eventually, her breathing slowed, and her lashes fluttered. I gathered her close as her muscles gave out, and she passed out in my arms with the sweetest little sigh I'd ever heard.

I wrapped myself around her like a damn blanket, one hand splayed protectively across her belly as if I could will life to begin inside her already.

Contentment settled over me. No matter what was happening in the world around us, in her arms, I found peace.

Then my phone buzzed.

Groaning, I stared at the ceiling, fighting the desire not to move.

But I didn't have a choice. I couldn't hold off on handling this shit. Not when I had something worth protecting.

Grabbing my phone, I checked the message.

FOX

All set for tomorrow night.

ME

Text me the details.

FOX

Will do. Be in my office two hours before you leave to go over last-minute shit.

ME

See you then.

I shut off the screen and tossed the phone on the nightstand, then tucked Lindsay even closer and let sleep take me.

Tomorrow, I'd walk into hell.

Tonight, I had heaven in my arms.

11

LINDSAY

I woke up wrapped in heat and muscle, my cheek pressed against Beck's bare chest. His arm was locked tightly around my waist as though I might vanish if he let go. For a guy who always looked like he was one second away from snarling at the world, he sure clung like a caveman in his sleep.

Not that I was complaining.

I didn't move right away. Last night had been a lot—chaos, danger, arguments, and multiple rounds of sex that had left me shaky in the best way. Waking up like this felt safe.

I hadn't known Beck long, but my body had apparently decided he was my personal security blanket. And my heart saw him as my forever.

Considering how many times he'd mentioned getting me pregnant, and that we'd never used a condom, I wanted to assume he felt the same way. But I was too scared to ask.

His voice rumbled low and rough beneath my cheek. "You awake?"

"Mmm," I hummed. "Thinking about going back to sleep. You make a really good pillow."

He snorted and brushed his lips against the top of my head. "Good thing I haven't gone down for coffee yet. Figured you'd want it fresh."

My eyes blinked open. "You waited?"

He shrugged as if it was no big deal. "Didn't want it gettin' cold if you were too busy hogging my bed to drink it."

I twisted around to grin up at him. "That's probably the nicest thing anyone's ever said to me first thing in the morning."

His chest shook as he chuckled. "'Cause I'm the only man you've woken up next to."

"Obviously." I stretched and kissed his jaw before slipping out of bed. "Lead the way, caveman. Now that I'm up, coffee first. Then maybe I'll forgive you for spanking me last night."

"You enjoyed every second of it," he muttered as he threw on a T-shirt and jeans.

Apparently worrying him meant getting spanked. Repeatedly. With zero regrets. On either of our parts.

When we got up to get dressed, I slipped on one of Beck's T-shirts and tied it at the waist before pulling on a pair of snug jeans. He had sent a prospect to grab some stuff for me while my mom was at work since it was safer for her if I stayed away until we figured this all out. So I had other stuff I could wear, but I liked being in his shirts...and the reaction I got from him.

His eyes raked over my outfit with heat and approval, making butterflies dance in my stomach. I was tempted to lure him back into bed, but I was starving, so we headed downstairs together. The clubhouse was already buzzing with quiet morning activity. A couple of men nodded to Beck as we passed, but most of the action was centered in the kitchen.

"There she is!" Dahlia called out, balancing a toddler on one hip while she stirred something on the stove. I met the club president's wife yesterday and had been amazed by how easily she seemed to handle being the mom of twins. "You hungry? Or just in desperate need of caffeine like the rest of us?"

Her daughter toddled over to us and lifted her

arms toward Beck. My heart melted when he bent low to pick up Violet and cradle her against his chest. Again, I was reminded of how he'd taken me without any protection. Every single time we'd had sex. And all the dirty talk about knocking me up.

We hadn't even put a name to our relationship or shared our feelings with each other yet—at least not in the form of those three little words—but it was easy to picture Beck holding our daughter sometime in the future.

Shaking my head to dispel the image, I beamed a smile at Dahlia. "Both. Definitely both."

"You're in luck." She handed Jett off to Fox after he strode into the kitchen. "Sadie left a few batches of cinnamon rolls in the fridge that I just had to pop in the oven."

I licked my lips. "Yum."

"Yummy," Violet echoed, making me laugh.

"Sounds like I'm not the only one looking forward to a delicious breakfast." I crossed the room to grab two mugs. After pouring coffee into both and adding cream to mine, I joined Beck at the table, where he had sat down with Violet on his lap.

"Thanks, baby."

Dahlia slid a plate of cinnamon rolls on the table in front of us. "Aw, so sweet."

"You sound like a sap," Savage muttered from the doorway, earning a glare from Beck.

"Careful how much shit you give me," Beck growled. "You know what they say about reaping what you sow."

"Sure turned out that way for you," Fox pointed out with a wide grin.

I mock-glared at Beck. "Why warn him when I'm the best darn thing that's ever happened to you?"

Dahlia laughed. "She's got you there."

Savage looked smug until Beck brushed a kiss against my cheek and taunted, "You'd be lucky as fuck to find a woman half as incredible as mine."

"Still sweet," Dahlia murmured with a grin.

Savage shook his head as he stalked over to the coffee pot. "And so fucking weird since Phoenix isn't known for his warm and cuddly personality."

Dahlia's smile disappeared when her daughter echoed, "Fuck."

"Watch your mouth." Fox slapped the back of Savage's head.

"Sorry," Savage muttered before keeping his mouth shut except for sipping his coffee and eating.

The rest of breakfast passed in a blur of caffeine, sticky fingers, and the kind of teasing that bounced from one end of the kitchen to the other. Nobody brought up business or me almost being kidnapped. Probably because we were all too busy cramming cinnamon rolls into our mouths to talk.

After the last roll disappeared and the kids toddled off for naps—or mayhem, depending on the family—we hung out with a couple of the guys and their pregnant wives in the great room. Beck didn't say much, just held my hand and rubbed lazy circles against my palm with his thumb as though he couldn't stand not touching me.

Later in the day, I kicked off my shoes and curled up sideways across the bed. He followed a second later, flopping down behind me and tugging me into his chest like I was the world's most valuable possession. One hand slid under my shirt, resting warm and possessive on my stomach.

At some point, I must've dozed off. The next thing I knew, the light outside had shifted to darkness and Beck was stroking a hand down my back in slow, unhurried lines.

"Hey," he said softly. "I have to head out for a bit."

I rolled over to face him, blinking the sleep from my eyes. "Now? Where?"

"Club business. Nothing you need to worry about," he reassured me.

I stared up at him, reading between the lines. He didn't tell me anything more. I'd seen the time and location in the notebook. I knew where he was going.

"You want me to stay here," I said slowly.

"You *will* stay here." He cupped my cheek, his thumb tracing a soft line beneath my eye, softening the steel behind his order. "I'll be back before you know it."

"Beck..."

He claimed my mouth in a deep kiss, swallowing my words. "Gotta keep you safe. You've already been targeted once. I'm not risking it again."

I swallowed hard and gave him a short nod even though every instinct I had screamed not to sit this one out.

He kissed me again, slow and lingering, then stood and grabbed his cut from the back of the chair.

"Be good," he murmured. "I'll be back before you know it."

And just like that, he was gone.

I stayed in Beck's room for about an hour after he left.

At first, I told myself I was doing what he asked. That I was being smart. Safe.

But the silence was deafening, and my thoughts were louder than ever. I stared at the notebook on the desk across the room like it might leap up and scream the truth at me.

I knew where he was going.

I'd decoded the location myself. I knew the exact time. I didn't even need GPS to find it with how good my memory was.

My fingers curled into fists as I stood, spine straightening. I was the one who'd brought this problem to Beck. I wasn't going to wait in a locked room like some princess in a tower while the people who hurt Paul—and tried to take me—walked free.

I understood why Beck wanted to protect me. But this wasn't about reckless defiance.

It was about closure.

So I grabbed Beck's extra cut and put it on over the shirt I'd borrowed this morning, then slipped into the hallway and closed the door behind me without a sound. The clubhouse was quieter now—muted voices from another room, the low hum of a TV.

I padded down the back staircase and went through a side door to the parking lot where my car was parked. I thought I was home free until I pulled up to the gate, and a prospect was staffing it.

He looked like I'd tossed him a live grenade when he spotted me in the driver's seat. "I don't know if I'm supposed to—uh—let you...I mean, Phoenix—"

I forced a soft smile. "I just forgot something I promised to grab for Beck earlier. Figured I'd run home really quick, so he's not going to be twice as grumpy tomorrow. Nobody wants that. Right?"

The kid paled. "No. Definitely not."

"Don't worry. I'll be back before anyone even notices I'm gone."

He hesitated for another second, then opened the gate with a heavy sigh.

I felt guilty for lying and hoped he didn't get into trouble for letting me out of the compound, but it didn't stop me from pulling onto the road with a single deep breath.

Twenty minutes later, I pulled into a gravel lot behind a strip of abandoned businesses on the edge of town. The windows were dark, the signage faded. Nothing looked active. But cars were clustered around one building in particular. Two men loitered near the side entrance, smoking.

My hands clenched around the steering wheel as I stared out the windshield. This might not have been my smartest move, but I already made it.

When Beck found me, he was going to be furious.

But I'd rather face his anger than live with the regret of sitting this one out. And if this gamble paid off, maybe I'd deliver answers this time.

12

PHOENIX

The warehouse was a forgotten skeleton of rust and shadows. The parking lot held plenty of vehicles, but it somehow still felt empty. They'd done a good job of picking somewhere isolated.

I clocked the muscle at the door as I approached. His eyes snagged on the Iron Rogues patch on my cut, and his posture shifted nervously. Then his spine straightened, chin tilting up with false bravado. But his eyes gave away his uncertainty, as though he wasn't sure if he should let me in or run for backup.

Smart bastard.

However, he didn't say anything and just opened the gate to let me inside.

The wide-open space was made of stained concrete, exposed steel beams, and a few overhead fluorescents flickering like they were seconds from dying. The air reeked of sweat and stale cigars, the smoke swirling in the air and adding to the haze caused by the shitty lighting. There was also a thick undercurrent of desperation.

The poker tables were set up in the middle of the floor, ringed by metal chairs that were occupied by every kind of lowlife you could imagine—ex-cons, dirty businessmen, dealers with twitchy eyes and guns tucked under their jackets.

More muscle patrolled the room, armed and threatening, making it clear that anyone who caused trouble would be dealt with in a way that would most likely involve pain and screaming. When I walked in, each one who looked my way had a similar reaction to the guy at the door. They took in my cut with the kind of hesitation that said they weren't sure if this was a warning shot from the club or I was just a biker who liked cards. Either way, they didn't want to make the wrong call, so no one stopped me from taking an empty chair.

I played a few rounds at one of the main tables, quiet and steady. Winning one and losing two, keeping my demeanor blank. Calm. Non-threatening. As much as I could be, considering my already intimidating stature and being an Iron Rogue. I was just another guy playing cards on a Saturday night. The others at the table kept glancing at my cut, trying to figure out if I was up to something, but I didn't give them anything.

Until Lindsay walked in.

My blood turned to ice and fire all at once. *Son of a fucking bitch!*

She wore my shirt under my spare cut, had her hair pulled up in a messy bun, and walked with her chin high. She looked every bit the confident woman who belonged to a ruthless biker. Every man in the room noticed her the second she stepped through the door, and my fingers itched to reach for my gun. I hated that any of these sleazy fuckers were looking at her, probably picturing my woman naked. But I somehow forced myself to remain composed.

What the fuck was she doing here?

Lindsay moved with a cool grace, like someone who knew she belonged anywhere she was. There was also that sweet sass in her step as she walked straight toward me, stopping at my side and pressing a kiss to my jaw like we hadn't just argued over this exact scenario. Clearly, her ass wasn't stinging enough from the last warning I'd given her.

"Hey," she purred, her voice teasing. "Sorry I'm late."

I stood and slid my hand around her wrist, tugging her flush against my chest. I let my fingers trail down her spine as I kissed her, making sure there was no mistaking who she belonged to. Then I bent to whisper in her ear. My voice was low and sharp as a blade when I hissed, "You won't be able to sit for a week after the spanking I'm gonna give you—for disobeying. For scaring the hell out of me by putting yourself in danger. I'm gonna light that pretty ass up until you're soaked and sobbing, and then I'm gonna fuck you so deep you'll feel me every time you breathe."

Her eyes went wide, and her cheeks flushed pink. But to her credit, she didn't miss a beat. Just gave me a coy little smile and perched herself on the arm of my chair as though she hadn't just signed her own death warrant.

I should've marched her out right then and there. But if I made a scene, we could blow up the whole plan. So I bit my tongue and sat back down.

With her subtle cues—nails tapping once, twice, then dragging on my shoulder—I started raking in the wins. Five hands in a row, cleaning out one guy. Then another. With each win, the dealer's lips thinned. Eventually, I spotted two men near the exit, hands at their sides, whispering to each other while stealing glances at Lindsay.

Fuck.

They weren't watching me.

They were watching her.

Shit. Shit. Shit. I couldn't fucking believe I didn't think about them recognizing her. My worry for her had distracted me, which was another reason I'd been so adamant that she stay away from the game.

One of the goons slipped away through a side door, and less than five minutes later, the other one came over to us. "Boss wants a word."

I leaned back casually. "We done playing?"

He didn't answer. Just nodded at two meatheads who were now approaching from behind him.

"She stays here," I said, still mild but with a thread of steel in my tone.

The bigger one, with a scar down his cheek and a jaw like a bulldog, shook his head. "Both of you. Now."

Lindsay tensed, but I gave her a quick squeeze at the waist as I stood. "Let's go."

We were led down a dark hallway and into a back office that looked more like a set from a mob movie than real life. The man behind the desk was huge, with dark beady eyes, a crooked nose, and a gold chain stretched tight over his thick neck. A pistol lay on the table in front of him, as though he wanted to make a point the loud way.

He didn't bother standing and eyed Lindsay with curiosity that made my fists twitch.

"Guess Paul's outta the picture, and you've already moved on. Good for you, sweetheart. Shame about the coma. Doesn't seem like you were together long, so I imagine he thought he'd cash in and maybe finally get a taste." He sneered, licking his teeth. "Course, cheating voids the winnings...but not the debt. That's yours now. One way or another."

His hungry eyes raked over her body, lingering on her tits and making it hard for me to keep from lunging across the desk and rip his throat out.

Lindsay blinked. "I don't—wait. Paul?" She cringed. "No. I've never...he was the manager of the Juniper Grove, where I volunteer. That's all. I barely know him."

He snorted. "That why you were at the hospital?"

"Yes, to tell him that we found out he was stealing from the center. Not for anything else," she said, disgust coloring her tone.

The boss looked at me then, his eyes cold. "And you? You walk in here like you own the room. As if you've got nothing to prove and nothing to lose. That's not how gamblers act. That's how sharks circle. It can only be one of two things—either you're cheating or you're sending a message. And I don't like either one."

I didn't speak, just continued to stare him down in silence.

"So here's how it's gonna go," he continued, his voice like gravel over broken glass. "You're gonna forget about your winnings. You're gonna disappear. But first, someone's gonna pay me what I'm owed. Since Paul's out cold, and this girl is on your arm now, that someone is you."

Lindsay shuffled closer to me, and I slipped my arm around her, resting my hand on her hip and giving it a reassuring squeeze.

"Don't give a fuck how you get it. You're the money guy, right? Treasurer for the Iron Rogues? Steal it from your club if you have to. But you've got two hours to come up with it." He jerked his chin toward Lindsay. "We'll hang on to your girl in the meantime. Call it insurance."

I went still, and the air in the room dropped several degrees.

"And if I don't?" I asked, voice low and flat.

He smirked. "Then she stays. As payment."

His eyes raked over Lindsay's body, slow and greasy. "She looks like a fighter, but they all beg eventually."

He leaned back and waved one of his goons forward. The guy reached for Lindsay, grabbing her arm as though he was about to yank her away.

That was when I moved.

I slammed my forearm into the bastard's throat, sending him crashing into the bookshelf behind him. Then I pulled my Glock and pressed it to the skull of the other asshole who'd made a move toward my woman.

"You touch her again," I growled, low and lethal, "and I will decorate this whole fucking room with your brains."

The boss slammed his chair back against the wall as he jumped to his feet. His eyes wide and furious. "You think you can threaten me? You think one MC pussy gets to come in here and make demands?"

My smile was pure ice. "Shoulda thought twice about running games in Iron Rogues' territory without permission. And thought even harder before you threatened my woman."

He laughed. "So what? What are you gonna do about it, motherfucker? You're outnumbered.

Outgunned. You walked in here with no backup and think I'm supposed to be scared?"

Everything paused when shouting started outside the room.

Then there was a bang. And another before the door burst open.

Fox sauntered in first, calm as hell. Maverick and Savage flanked him, both holding suppressed weapons with casual ease.

The guy I'd flattened was back on his feet, and he rushed over, grabbing Lindsay and spinning her around before putting a gun to her head.

Fox didn't flinch. He just raised a brow.

"Suggest you let her go," Fox drawled. "Or they'll be digging your teeth out of the floorboards."

The boss snarled, shoving his desk aside and pointing a pistol at my chest. "You think I won't do it? Get the fuck out before I put your accountant in the ground."

Fox chuckled, slow and deadly as he walked over to stand just beside the fucker's desk. "Really don't get it, do you?" He looked at Lindsay, then back at the boss. "You don't see the storm you just stepped into. Bastards who touch what's not theirs—especially when it belongs to an Iron Rogue—have issued their own death sentence."

Maverick smirked and added, "And you've seriously underestimated what Phoenix is capable of."

My eyes locked with Lindsay's, and when she nodded, I took that moment of distraction to move. She ducked, fast and smooth, and I shot the bastard behind her in the shoulder. He screamed and dropped the gun as he staggered backward. Then I rushed forward and cracked the guy's skull against the wall with the butt of my weapon.

At the same time, Fox had stepped toward the boss and slammed the guy's face into the table with one fluid motion as he disarmed him.

Savage had dropped the last guy before he could aim.

And Maverick had grabbed the guy who'd rushed into the room, breaking his neck with ease, before tossing him to the ground.

The whole thing took under five seconds.

Brutal, but efficient.

Maverick appeared at my side, watching me, waiting for permission. I was reluctant to let Lindsay go, but I didn't want her seeing what happened next. I nodded, and he took her elbow, turning her toward the door. She opened her mouth to argue but shut it when she saw the look on my face.

Once she was gone from the room, Fox

squeezed the back of the boss's neck and pulled him up, the barrel of his gun digging into the shithead's back.

The boss's nose was spurting blood, clearly broken, and from the look of it, his right cheekbone was shattered.

I pointed my Glock at his forehead and growled, "You're not gonna like what comes next."

Savage snorted a laugh. "No one ever does."

Aiming my gun again, I pulled the trigger, putting a bullet right between his legs. The pussy screamed like a little girl, tears running down his face as he begged me to let him go.

"Nobody fucks with an Iron Rogue, motherfucker," Fox snarled.

The next shot was straight through the heart.

I didn't wait for anything else before I spun around and made a beeline out the door. Once I was in the mostly empty front room—with the exception of a few other Rogues—I spotted my woman near the front entrance. She was pacing anxiously, her hands rubbing her arms for warmth.

I stalked over and pulled Lindsay against me. Her breath hitched as she buried her face against my chest.

"Go," Maverick murmured. "Got this handled."

I lifted my chin in thanks, then moved Lindsay to my side, keeping her plastered up against me.

"Let's go. Before I put another bullet in someone else." I growled, dragging her out of the room and into the lot where our bikes and the club's backup vehicles were parked.

Lindsay tried to speak as we approached my hog, but I cut her off with a glare.

She swallowed hard. "I'm sorry."

I shook my head, jaw clenched so tight it ached. "Your apology won't take away the fear I felt seeing a gun to your head."

"I know—"

"And it sure as hell won't save you from the permanent handprint I'm gonna leave on your pretty little ass."

She didn't argue.

Smart girl.

I put my helmet on her head, then scooped her up and deposited her onto the back of my bike.

As we rode back to the compound, my blood was still boiling, my hands shaking. I didn't know how long it was gonna take before I stopped imagining every worst-case scenario that could have played out.

But I was gonna fuck my girl deep and hard, over

and over, until I was convinced that she was safe in my arms.

13

LINDSAY

The drive back to the clubhouse was tense. Not that I could blame him for being pissed.

I'd defied him. Put myself in danger. Drawn attention. And even if I hadn't totally screwed everything up, I knew I'd crossed a line.

But even with all that, if I had the chance to do it all over again, I would probably make the same decision.

The clubhouse loomed ahead, the parking lot mostly empty aside from a few bikes and a pair of trucks parked near the side. Beck pulled into his usual spot and killed the engine of his bike without looking at me.

My stomach flipped as he lifted me off the motorcycle and took my hand in a firm grip before stalking toward the front door. I followed him without a word.

The second we stepped inside, the energy shifted. Conversations stopped and heads turned.

No one said anything, but they all watched us.

Beck didn't slow down. He walked me straight through the main room, his hand wrapped around mine in a grip I couldn't have broken even if I tried.

My cheeks were burning, and not just from embarrassment. It was also anticipation.

I'd seen that look in Beck's eyes when he realized I'd followed him. I wasn't going to get yelled at.

I was going to get spanked. And judging by his silence and the tension still radiating off him as we climbed the stairs, I wasn't getting off lightly.

When we stepped into his room, he shut the door behind us with a soft click. Then he turned and flipped the lock.

Beck didn't say a word. He just stalked across the room to the chair and sat down like a man preparing for battle. His eyes found mine—and I froze at the dangerous look in his hazel orbs.

"Over here," he said, voice low.

My feet moved before my brain caught up to his command. The quiet rasp of my shoes on the hardwood was the only sound as I crossed the room.

When I reached him, he didn't yank me into place. He just held my gaze.

"You scared the fuck out of me, baby."

My breath caught. "I know."

"You don't get to do that again."

"I'll try my best," I promised.

His eyes darkened. "Then I guess I better make sure you remember this."

Before I could respond, he caught my wrist and gently but firmly tugged me over his lap and yanked down my jeans and panties. His palm smoothed over the curve of my butt once, then he smacked me before I had the chance to tense.

I gasped, more from the shock than the sting.

"One for sneaking out when I told you to stay put for your own safety," he murmured, hand smoothing again. "Another for lying to the prospect at the gate and putting his future as an Iron Rogue at risk by making him believe your bullshit."

Swat.

"A couple more for putting yourself in danger."

He gave me a smack to each cheek this time.

His hand paused, resting there as though he needed to anchor himself. Then it lifted again. "And one for scaring the fuck outta me."

The last swat made me squirm, and not just from the heat blooming on my skin.

"You're such a caveman," I mumbled into his lap.

He tsked as he pulled my pants back over my butt. "Didn't hear a thank you, baby."

"As if," I huffed, even though my panties were already soaked from the spanking I'd more than earned.

A low growl rumbled in his chest. One second, I was across his lap, and the next, I was airborne—landing on the mattress with Beck looming over me, eyes lit with fire. "After what happened tonight, you're sassing me already?"

I shrugged. "Someone's gotta keep you on your toes."

"You keep running that mouth"—he pressed his hips down against mine—"and I'll remind you who it belongs to."

I arched under him with a moan, heat surging low in my belly.

He kissed me hard and deep, his weight holding me down in the best way as his hands explored with the same kind of rough tenderness I was already addicted to.

When he finally pulled back, I was breathless, aching, and absolutely ready for more. Unfortunately, someone had the worst timing and knocked on the door.

"Fucking hell," Beck groaned, dropping his forehead against mine.

"Hate to interrupt, but I figured you'd want that thing I sent out for as soon as it came back," Fox explained through the door. "Leavin' it in the hallway for you."

I had no clue what he was talking about, but it spurred Beck to crawl off me and stride across the room.

He yanked the door open, bent down, and picked up a small bundle left just outside in the hallway. Then he kicked the door shut behind him, his movements still sharp—like he hadn't fully come down from the adrenaline high yet. But something in his eyes had shifted when he turned back to me.

Satisfaction gleamed from the hazel depths.

I sat up on the mattress, tugging the hem of my shirt down, but I didn't bother trying to look innocent. It was a little late for that.

He crossed the room and dropped onto the edge of the bed in front of me. "I should probably wait to do this somewhere nice, not right after spanking your perfect ass pink."

I quirked a brow. "That doesn't sound like us."

His mouth twitched. "So fucking perfect for me."

He dropped the bundle into my lap. My breath caught when I saw what it was—a leather cut, smaller than his, and with a patch across the back that said Property of Phoenix.

"You really..." I whispered, fingers shaking as I touched the patch.

"Yeah." His voice was low. "You're mine, baby. Now nobody can miss it."

My throat tightened, tears prickling at the corners of my eyes before I could stop them. I looked up at him, trying to blink them back.

"I love you," I breathed. "So much."

He leaned in, slid his hand into my hair, and kissed me like the words undid something in him. When he pulled back, his hazel eyes burned into mine.

"Fuck, I love you. And I want you by my side every damn day. So I'm not just giving you a patch." He reached into the top drawer of his bedside table and pulled out a small black box. "I'm also giving you this."

My heart skipped as he opened it. There was a ring inside. He went classic—a solitaire diamond, gold band, all simple elegance. Like he somehow knew that underneath the sass, I wanted something that would still make me cry.

"Be my old lady. My wife. The mother of my kids. The reason I don't burn the damn world down when it pisses me off."

I let out a teary laugh and nodded so fast I probably looked ridiculous. "Yes. Yes to all of it."

He slipped the ring on my finger, then leaned in for another kiss—this one softer, slower, but no less claiming.

When he lifted his head again, I looked down at my hand. I couldn't stop staring at the ring. It felt a little surreal to have something so perfect on my finger.

Beck sat behind me, his arms wrapped around my waist as I leaned back against his chest on the bed. His chin rested on my shoulder, and we were both quiet, soaking the moment in. He kissed the side of my neck, his scruff dragging just enough to make me shiver. "I have one more thing for you."

I tilted my head. "You do?"

"It's not shiny." His voice dropped, thoughtful. "But I figured you might want it anyway."

I turned to look at him, one brow lifting. "Okay..."

"The community center's not closing," he said.

"Fox and I talked, and we've got the additional funding covered to keep the place going. We're gonna overhaul it—fix the shit that's broken, bring in real support. But we need someone we can trust to run it."

My heart skipped. "You want me to run the center?"

"I can't imagine anyone else taking Paul's place." He tucked a strand of hair behind my ear. "You love those kids. That place made you. It deserves someone who gets that."

I blinked quickly, trying not to cry again. "I already checked to see if I could switch to all online classes this fall. I was having a hard time picturing myself being away from Old Bridge for almost two whole years while I finished my degree. I might have to drive up there for exams every once in a while, but my adviser assured me it was possible to finish the rest of my classes from here."

His eyes lit with happiness. "You were planning for us?"

"Of course I was." I turned in his arms, pressing my hand against his chest. "So were you."

He kissed me again, slower this time. Sweeter. And when he pulled back, his smile was soft but sure. "You walked into my life swinging, baby. And I knew right then you were gonna knock me on my ass."

I grinned. "Good. Because I don't plan on going easy on you anytime soon."

"Wouldn't want you to."

I curled deeper into his arms, the ring on my finger catching the light as I finally let myself relax.

I'd walked into the clubhouse looking for answers. Instead, I found everything I didn't know I needed.

EPILOGUE
PHOENIX

"You doing okay, baby?" I asked softly, rubbing a hand over Lindsay's belly.

She nodded and leaned back in the booth, stretching her legs out to prop them on the bench seat across from us.

Since she had the day off from the center, she'd come with me to the bar owned by the club, Midnight Rebel. I was balancing the books with Savage since he managed the place.

"Can I get you anything?" I asked my wife.

"Um, a foot rub?" she suggested hopefully.

I chuckled and kissed her temple. "The second we get home."

Savage had pulled up a chair to the end of the booth and was watching our interaction with a smirk.

"What?" I growled.

He shrugged. "Just never thought I'd see you go so soft."

I rolled my eyes. "Only for her. And our kids. Everyone else? Still gets a bullet."

Savage snorted.

"You'll see," I predicted before turning back to the numbers.

When a cool breeze came in, I glanced up and a wide smile broke over my face.

My eighteen-year-old sister, Melanie, walked inside, followed by another girl who looked to be a similar age.

"Bro!" she screeched, running over to throw herself into my arms the second I was on my feet.

"Hey, kid," I greeted her, kissing the top of her head as I gave her a squeeze.

Then I pulled back and frowned down at her. "What the fuck, Lainie?" I grunted. "You didn't tell me you were coming."

"I wanted to surprise you," she chirped happily as she pushed me out of the way to climb into the booth to hug my woman.

The other girl was hanging back, looking around nervously. She looked innocent and downright wholesome, so I figured all the tatted, rugged bikers were probably freaking her out.

Not wanting my sister's friend to feel unwelcome, I smiled and held out my hand. "Hey. I'm Lainie's brother, Phoenix."

Before our hands touched, Savage was standing between us, his chair crashing to the floor from standing up so fast.

"That's Savage," I muttered.

"Talon," he corrected, telling her his first name.

My brow shot up.

"Um, Tamara," she replied softly.

"We need your help," Lainie said as she climbed back out of the booth.

I was about to respond, but Savage cut me off.

"Let's go to my office," he suggested. From his tone, it didn't sound like a request.

He grabbed Tamara's hand and marched toward the door that led to the back of the bar.

Lanie glanced up at me curiously, but I just shrugged, so she sighed and scampered after her friend.

"This is going to be interesting," Lindsay said, her voice filled with mirth.

"Yeah," I agreed as I turned around. I snapped my laptop shut, knowing Savage was gonna be too occupied to finish the books for a while. "Let's get you home for that foot rub."

LINDSAY GROANED SOFTLY and shifted on the bed, trying to find a position that didn't have her wincing. She was all curves and glow and softness. Her belly was round with our baby, and her legs were tangled in the sheets. My shirt barely fit over the swell of her stomach, and I loved it. Seeing the proof that she was mine, that I'd done my fucking job and bred my woman—like the caveman she accused me of being.

"You need me, baby?" I asked, watching her with sympathy.

Her frustrated sigh punched straight into my chest. "I just can't get comfortable."

I was across the room in two strides, kneeling on the mattress beside her. "Roll toward me."

She did so slowly, and I slipped a pillow between her knees. Then I climbed onto the bed and lay down behind her. I cupped her belly, holding her close and kissing her shoulder. "There. Better?"

"Mmm. Yeah."

I stroked a hand over her side. "I can make it even better."

She let out a soft laugh. "I bet you can." Then she paused, and her voice was soft and sweet when she added, "He kicked earlier. When I said your name."

My heart nearly stopped. "He did?"

"He knows you already."

I dropped my forehead against her back and let out a breath that shook. My hand splayed even wider, possessively over her belly. When I felt another little thump under my hand, I nearly forgot how to breathe.

Lindsay's eyes shimmered as she looked back at me over her shoulder. "You okay?"

I nodded slowly. "More than okay." I bent down and kissed her shoulder, then her lips. "You're in our bed, wearing my ring, carrying our kid." I kissed her neck again, rougher this time. "And you still don't understand how deep this runs, do you?"

Lindsay turned in my arms and kicked the pillow away. Her breath caught as I pushed the hem of my shirt up and kissed the top of her bump.

"I'm fucking obsessed with you," I murmured, brushing my mouth along her skin.

She bit her lip, and her breath caught as my hands slid along her thighs.

"You like being mine?" I asked softly. "Letting

me take care of you, keep you safe, put this baby in you?"

She nodded, cheeks flushed. "Yes."

I tucked a strand of hair behind her ear, then lowered my voice, teasing, "Next time? Maybe I'll go for twins."

"Oh good grief. I'd be huge!" she muttered.

"Gorgeous," I corrected.

She gave a half laugh, half moan as I kissed her again, and her hands fisted in my shirt. The kiss was slow and hot and aching.

Eventually, her fingers tangled in my hair, and she tugged hard. I pulled back just enough to look into her eyes with a smirk. "You want me, baby?"

"I always want you," she whimpered.

That was all I needed.

I helped her onto her back, being careful with her belly, then slid her panties down her legs and tossed them aside. She was already warm, soft, and wet for me. My woman always was.

I spread her thighs gently and settled between them, brushing my nose along her inner thigh before kissing her center.

She gasped and gripped the sheets as I licked her slow and deep. I worshipped her. Ate her until she was shaking, until her hips were arching off the bed and her fingers were buried in my hair.

"You're perfect," I rasped, dragging my tongue over her again. "Everything about you."

When she came, she cried out my name like it was the only word she knew.

I moved up her body, kissing her belly, her breasts, her mouth, and finally slid my throbbing dick inside her with one deep, hard thrust.

"Beck!" she screamed, sending shock waves of bliss through my body.

She was tight as fuck and still trembling from the aftershocks of her first climax.

I held myself above her as I rocked into her with slow, deliberate movements—like every thrust was a promise.

I kept my eyes locked with hers so I could see her passion as it grew, and my name left her lips in a ragged whisper, begging for more.

"This is where you're meant to be," I murmured. "Under me. Around me. Full of me."

Her eyes fluttered closed, and I kissed her again, deeper this time, until we were both breathless.

"I'm gonna give you everything," I growled softly. "More babies. A home. A life you never dreamed of."

She moaned, her nails biting into my back. And when she came again, she clenched around me, milking my cock so I followed with a groan so deep it felt like it was ripped from my soul.

Afterward, I wrapped myself around her, one hand splayed over her belly like a shield.

I couldn't stop touching her.

Because she was everything—my woman, my future, my family.

The woman who owned every piece of me, and I planned to keep her close for the rest of my life.

EPILOGUE
LINDSAY

After three years of planning, I never thought this day would come. The new community center gleamed in the sunlight—all fresh paint, polished windows, and possibilities. The building was much bigger than the old one. And brighter too, but it still felt like home.

Which made sense, considering how much of my heart lived inside these walls. The rest of it was sitting in the audience, beaming big smiles at me.

I stood on the small stage in front of the new entryway, my hand resting on the curve of my very pregnant belly as I looked out over the crowd. Kids I'd watched grow up were bouncing with excitement. Volunteers, staff, and parents filled the rows of folding chairs. Off to the side, a wall of men in leather cuts stood watch, their arms crossed and sunglasses hiding expressions that were probably a little too soft for their reputations. Their wives and children were in the crowd of seated people as well.

Beck sat front and center, holding our daughter in one arm while our son clung to his leg. Baxter had his eyes. Laura had my sass. And both of them had our entire world wrapped around their fingers. Their grandmother's too.

My mom sat to Beck's right, an empty chair on her other side that we all knew my son wouldn't use. If he got tired of standing, Baxter would crawl into my mom's lap instead.

Meeting Beck's eyes, I blew him a quick kiss. Then I took a few deep breaths to calm my nerves before tapping the microphone to get everyone's attention. "I want to thank you all for being here today. When I was a kid, this place was a second home for me. It gave me safety, support, and snacks I didn't have to share with anyone."

Laughter rippled through the crowd.

"And now? It's where I get to give all that back. To see this place standing stronger than ever—full of light, life, laughter—that's not something I could've imagined when the Iron Rogues asked me to step in as the manager six years ago. But here we are. And I'm grateful every day for the people who made this possible."

I glanced at Beck. Then June. And the kids crowded around the bounce house in the back. My voice thickened. "Because of all of you...this isn't just a building. It's hope. And it's home."

Applause erupted, and I smiled through the lump in my throat.

After the ribbon was cut and the formalities were done, I stepped off the stage. Slowly, thanks to the watermelon masquerading as my stomach. I felt Beck's arm wrap around my waist before my feet even touched the sidewalk.

"I said I wouldn't hover," he muttered against my temple. "But you're carrying my kid and standing on a stage. That's testing me, baby."

"You're lucky I didn't trip over the mic cord," I teased. "I could've gone down like a sack of potatoes."

"Don't even joke about shit like that," he growled under his breath. Then he pressed a kiss to my shoulder before looking down at our daughter. "Your mommy is a menace."

"No," she disagreed with a grin. "Mommy da boss."

"Damn right she is," a voice rasped behind me.

I turned to find June, still wearing the same faded volunteer tee she'd had the day I returned to the center during my summer break. Her smile was gentle, eyes glinting with emotion.

"You saved this place." She sniffled. "You really did."

"It saved me first," I whispered, pulling her in for a hug.

The celebration swirled around us. Someone had started a pickup soccer game on the new field, and the scent of barbecue and kettle corn filled the air. Balloons bounced along the pavement, sticky hands reached for cookies, and toddlers tottered between picnic tables under the watchful eyes of bikers.

And in the middle of it all, I stood with the man who'd claimed me, the babies we'd made, and another on the way. Beck didn't just protect me. He gave me a place to land after a lifetime of standing on my own.

I'd walked into the Iron Rogues' compound years ago full of fire and fury, ready to accuse their treasurer of negligence. Instead, I found a partner. A protector. My forever.

Savage isn't going to waste a minute to claim Tamara as his own!

And if you join our newsletter, you'll get a FREE copy of The Virgin's Guardian, which was banned on Amazon.

ABOUT THE AUTHOR

The writing duo of Elle Christensen and Rochelle Paige team up under the Fiona Davenport pen name to bring you sexy, insta-love stories filled with alpha males. If you want a quick & dirty read with a guaranteed happily ever after, then give Fiona Davenport a try!

Printed in Great Britain
by Amazon

62673326R00090